SECOND BURIAL

FOR A

BLACK PRINCE

SECOND BURIAL

FOR A

BLACK PRINCE

ANDREW NUGENT

THOMAS DUNNE BOOKS
ST. MARTIN'S MINOTAUR
NEW YORK

THOMAS DUNNE BOOKS.
An imprint of St. Martin's Press.

SECOND BURIAL FOR A BLACK PRINCE. Copyright © 2006 by Andrew Nugent. All rights reserved. Printed in the United States of America. No part of this book may be used or reproduced in any manner whatsoever without written permission except in the case of brief quotations embodied in critical articles or reviews. For information, address St. Martin's Press, 175 Fifth Avenue, New York, N.Y. 10010.

www.minotaurbooks.com

Library of Congress Cataloging-in-Publication Data

Nugent, Andrew.
    Second burial for a black prince / Andrew Nugent.— 1st ed.
        p. cm.
    ISBN-13: 978-0-312-32761-3
    ISBN-10: 0-312-32761-7
        1. Nigerians—Ireland—Fiction. 2. Blacks—Ireland—Fiction. 3. Immigrants—Ireland—Fiction. 4. Amputation—Fiction. 5. Brothers—Death—Fiction. 6. Police—Ireland—Dublin—Fiction. 7. Dublin (Ireland)—Fiction.
    I. Title.
    PR6114.U36S43 2006
    823'.92—dc22

                                                                    2006041120

First Edition: July 2006

10 9 8 7 6 5 4 3 2 1

The Ethiopians are said to be the most just of people, and for that reason the gods leave their abode frequently to visit them.

—LACTANTIUS PLACIDUS (VITH CENTURY A.D.)*

*Quoted from *Blacks in Antiquity: Ethiopians in the Greco-Roman Experience*, by Frank M. Snowden, Jr. (Harvard U.P., 1970)

ACKNOWLEDGMENTS

Sincere thanks to Ruth Cavin, Toni Plummer,
Carly Sommerstein, and Kevin Sweeney,
who so routinely saved me
from myself.

The second burial is not a literal reinterment.
It is that process by which the spirit of an African is laid to rest
and reuinted with the ancestors of the people.

SECOND BURIAL

FOR A

BLACK PRINCE

CHAPTER ONE

CLICK! ON, THE FRONT PORCH SECURITY LIGHT. *CLICK!* Open, the distrustful eye of Mary Murtagh upstairs in her bed.

"Jack, wake up, Jack, will you? There is somebody down at the door."

The doorbell rang, making an honest woman of her.

"Jack!"

"Sweet Jesus, Mary, what time is it?"

"Ten after two."

Another hawk of the bell, like a whiskey cough in the night.

"Get up, Jack, in the name of God!"

"I'll do anything within reason, ma'am, but I won't get up out of this bed."

She dumped herself heavily onto the floor. Flat-foot patter over to the window, screwing her face into focus. Clunk of a skull on the window pane. Rales of labored breathing.

"Merciful hour, Jack, it's a black man!"

"Sure, the King of the Congo. You're dreaming, woman!"

"Black as yer boot, Jack, I swear to God. Oh Jesus, he's blood all over, Jack, and he's falling down. Get up, Jack!"

Sergeant Molly Power belonged to the Murder Squad of the Garda Síochána, the Irish Police Force: in literal translation, the Guardians of the Peace. It was March and peace was doing fine: business was not brisk. Perhaps, the Irish being very religious, the assassins had given up murder for Lent. So Molly, all out of murders, was being usefully redeployed in patrol cars. It was four o'clock in the morning. She had been useful since midnight, being driven around the South Dublin seaboard by Garda Tommy O'Brien, instead of being at home asleep in the arms of Jan-Hein Van Zeebroeck, her darling young Dutch art-expert husband of nearly nine months whom she still loved frantically and forever.

The shift was midnight to 6:00 A.M. Midweek in March, not much had been happening. A break-in at an off-license in Dun Laoghaire. A maternity false alarm at Glenageary—wind probably, Molly thought. Then a handful of raucous teenagers to be dispersed from under somebody's window. These were young and not drunk. Mere sight of the police car was enough to send them scuttling home to their mummies. Most trouble had been an alleged suicide off the east pier, who turned out to be a bona fide midnight nippy-dipper with attitude, lots of attitude. They had stood on the windswept pier for forty minutes discussing the American Constitution and FDR's Four Freedoms, one of which, apparently, covered nude bathing in the dark.

The radio crackled.

"One-sixty, where are you?"

"One-sixty here. Killiney Hill," O'Brien answered.

"Good. Make for Loughlinstown Hospital, okay? Something about an African guy attacked. Bad scene. Sawed his leg off, or something."

"Jesus, tonight!" He looked at Molly. She nodded.

"Peel right, Tommy. We're on it, Control. Okay. Out."

She was with him when he died, vaguely hoping to get a statement. A nice-looking boy, about her own age, gentle, brave, so very lonely, full of faith. It affected her deeply.

Midmorning.

"Cut the leg off him, Inspector, and dumped him on the Dublin Mountains. I don't know how he got as far as that house."

"Was he conscious, Doctor?"

"When he got here, hardly. Said his name, Chat or Chad or something. That's all. He was dead in a few hours. Loss of blood. Irreversible shock. I'd say the shock was as much moral as physical. Just the horror of what had happened to him. I let your girl go in to him. I doubt if she got anything."

Inspector Jim Quilligan shook his head, phewing out vapors of disapproval.

"This racism is getting out of hand."

"Not racism, Inspector, not this time."

"Not racism! Hack the leg off a black man, and it's not racism?"

"There was no hacking. This leg was surgically removed, under anesthetic. A meticulous amputation below the knee joint. Racists don't give anesthetics, Inspector."

"Well, what the hell is this about?"

"You tell me, Inspector. The whole thing is weird. The operation, the amputation, was competently done. But whoever did the postoperative bit didn't have a bull's notion. A Boy Scout would have done better. The leg was ligatured crudely, the stump stuck into a black plastic bag, which was tied tightly at the top of the thigh. Then the chap was driven up the Dublin Mountains and dumped. He hadn't a hope."

Quilligan pulled his big hands down each side of his face.

"So the ligaturing and black bagging had nothing to do with recovery or recuperation. It was done just to stop the victim from bloodying up somebody's carpet or car."

The doctor looked at the inspector with interest.

"I suppose that has to be right. And, mind you, in that grisly perspective, the job was not so incompetent after all. Quite effective, I'd say, though the guy was pretty bloodied up by the time we saw him. But that probably happened after he was dumped, when he was struggling to get to that house. The plastic bag got torn, and some of the surgical stuff around the stump had come undone. The main artery was still holding, though. Otherwise he would have died long before he got here."

"Well, the dumping bit, at least: that has got to be racism."

"Or worse."

"What is worse than racism?"

The doctor shrugged.

"What you can't name is always worse."

"Was the severed bit, the foot, the foreleg, or whatever you call it, was it in the bag?"

"No. So riddle me that one. They keep his foot and they dump the rest of him. It's like what Gladstone said about Disraeli."

"What did he say?"

"You don't want to know."

Quilligan nodded slowly.

"Well, we'd better start finding out who he is, or was. Chad or Chat, you say—his name?"

"Yes, but I can do better. He had handbills in his pocket, ads for some sort of ethnic eating house. In Parnell Street, I think."

"Ah, Little Africa. That figures."

"Yes. Hold on there a moment."

The doctor went out and came back in a few minutes with a green plastic bag.

"We've left the clothes on him for the moment. They'll cut them off for the autopsy."

Quilligan winced, knowing how much else they would cut.

"But here's what was in the pockets: a Biro, some money, a comb—fuzzy hair, what do they need a comb for?—and the flyers."

Quilligan took one and flattened it out in his big hands. It was a hopeful little piece, badly printed on cheap paper.

COME TO:

SHAD'S PLACE

IGBO QUISINE

HAVE BIG MEAL EVERYTIME

RICE	AND	**R**
STEW		**S**
VERY		**V**
PLENTY		**P**

TRY OUR SOUPES: OKORO, EGUSI, OGBONOR, BITTER-LEAF

COME TO OUR RESTAURANT: **IT SERVES YOU RIGHT**!

FOOD READY EVERYTIME

4A PARNELL CLOSE, DUBLIN CITY N°1, IRELAND, EUROPE.

Quilligan could not help chuckling at "It serves you right" and at the sheer imagination displayed by turning a postal code into a quality rating. He gestured sadly even as he chuckled.

"God love him, and is this the best we can do for himself and the likes of him? Imagine coming all that way from Africa, just to die in a ditch like that. What age was he?"

The doctor forebore to point out that Loughlinstown Hospital is hardly a ditch. "Probably twenty-seven, twenty-eight, less than thirty anyhow. Go and see him yourself in the morgue, Inspector. He looks nice."

It was, Quilligan thought, a strange remark for a leathery old doctor.

At 3:00 A.M. Jude had slept for an hour, worn out finally from crying. Shad dead! Shadrack his brother, his senior one, his little father. He could not take it in. Shad was dead. How cold the bed was without him, how desolate the world, and how bitter this cruel little island of Ireland.

Jude Ekemauche Okafor: Igbo by tribe, native of Nnewi, Anambra State, Nigeria. Twenty-three years of age, about. White people always wanted exact figures. Why? What use was it? He did not know his mathematical age. He knew his age group. "The gazelles" they were called: wonder boys all of them, dancers, drummers, runners, tumblers, fleet and beautiful. Oh, where were they all now, Chinedu, Oneyma, Uchedike, Chidebere, the ever-faithful ones, the good, where were they now, his brothers, when, like a wounded warrior, he needed them and their strong arms to hold him up? And what of his mother, who would tell her? How would they tell her? She would die of grief, surely, for Shad—Nwachukwu—her first-born son.

In a stupor of grief and exhaustion, Jude saw Shad again in that hospital morgue where the police had brought him. So small he had seemed, so slender, motionless; the alive so dead, his mutilated body so pitiable in its torn, blood-stained clothes. He could hear Shad crying to him now, pleading, pleading: Shad, the strong one, the senior brother who always gave to his junior ones, Shad who never took anything for himself, how had he become so weak, so poor, so pitiously helpless?

Wide awake suddenly, terrified, he was lying flat on his face, as if for judgment, naked as for sacrifice, his sweat surging in the pulsating heat of the sacred forest. In his flared nostrils, that acrid tang, as unmistakable as his own smell, the animate musk of Africa, whose red earth he could feel gripping and throbbing beneath his drenched and trembling body. In his ears, drumbeats, night sounds of the deep forest, ecstasies and agonies of the hunt and of the dying, of rutting and killing.

The spirits were calling him, his father, his father's father, great elders before whom he had prostrated himself as a child, the heros of his race, many of their names forgotten or known only to priests or to the great storytellers, yet ever-present in his own life, to judge, to punish, or at times to reward honor, courage, and fidelity. These, the great ancestors of his Igbo clan and tribe, warriors and wizards, prophets and princes, saints, stern, inflexible men: these were calling to him now, to him by name: *Jude Ekemauche*. It was a great and terrible privilege, one rarely given and which could not be refused. In this night, his life was being utterly changed, his destiny was being written now forever, for better or for worse, for salvation or damnation.

"Ekemauche, our son, open your ears and listen. Attend to the voice of the spirits. You must lay this your brother, Nwachukwu, our son, to rest with honor. You must bring justice down on the heads of his murderers. Avenge this treacherous deed! Avenge the name of our people! Eat fire, Ekemauche! Drink deep of anger! May Great Chukwu strengthen your arm against our foes. May he enflame your *chi* with pitiless knowledge of all who talk lie, may he fill your belly with the valor of our greatest warriors.

"We command you, Ekemauche, choose now. Become a mighty one of our race, our blessed son, champion of the people—or else, be you ten times accursed and outcast forever."

Jude covered his head and ears with both hands, crushing his face down onto the earth in a gesture of intense fear, in supplication, in perfect submission.

It was already after eight o'clock when Jude woke from a deep dreamless sleep. Fresh fruit, fish, and vegetables were his responsibility, and he had never before missed the market. Downstairs he could hear Margot, their massive Ghanaian mum-away-from-mum, bustling between dining room and kitchen. She was doing, he did not doubt, Shad's work, and his, as well as her own.

Nothing could stop Margot. Besides feeding half the African population on Dublin's north side, she was universal mother to throngs of harried and lonely people, most of them black. It was she who had taken Jude in her arms the night before when the police had brought him back from identifying Shad's body. She had just sat for so long, holding him, stroking his head, singing soft songs in his ear, words which he could not understand, yet song that soothed his aching heart.

He lay on his back thinking, hands entwined behind his head. In one terrible night, he had ceased to be a child and had become a man, a man deeply sorrowing, yet calm now and strong, a man raised above mere self-pity and able to carry his pain. A man, too, who had pledged his deepest self. He would die rather than fail.

He got up and took his bath in a bucket of cold water, in traditional African style. Pure pleasure in the tropics: harsh penance in this unending Irish winter. But there was no money to spare for heating water.

As he washed, he reflected. Until four months before, Jude had never been farther than Anambra and the neighboring Igbo states, what used to be called Biafra. He spoke Igbo fluently and English well, but it was the English of Igboland and the Delta, quite different in syntax and intonation to the provincial dialects of Dublin. He had a big problem of communication in a city whose natives seemed certain that the best, indeed the only correct English in the world, was as spoken by themselves.

Jude was no stranger to city living. He knew Onitsha like the back of his hand and he had spent three months in Lagos on his way to Ireland. Anyone who survives those maelstroms, friends had assured him, would survive anywhere in the world. Dublin by comparison was small, and calm to the point of being eerie. He could not quite believe it at first: the cars stayed on their own side of the road—the wrong side actually—and they always stopped at red lights, even when there was no Yellow Fever man standing by with his whip to torture the drivers, as there was at home.

He still felt far from secure. Although not particularly hassled by police or immigration officials, most of whom seemed quite human, he had far too much to do with them. Visa offices to visit, police stations to report to, forms to fill out, questions to be answered, all the time more and more questions, many that he had no idea how to answer. Immigration formalities were interminable, bewildering, and intimidating. From day to day, from week to week, he had no idea whether his case for a resident's permit was going forward or backward. There was the nagging fear all the time that they would come for him suddenly and send him packing.

Perhaps now, with his brother dead, they would think that he was trouble and a bringer of bad luck. They would drive him out. Besides, he had no money to pay bribes. Always when tragedy strikes the police are involved, and when the police get involved, you have to *bring money*. Whether you are wrong or in the right, the police must *eat money*. Jude's own father had been struck and killed by a taxi. His family were poor people. The police would not let his family have the body to bury until they bring money. Eventually, one reverend sister "dashed" them two thousand *naira*. Their father stank at his funeral. Well, Shadrack would not stink at his funeral. Even if Jude had to kill for it, Shad would have a decent funeral. "Standard," as they say at home, by which they mean "the best."

Jude knew the world of Dublin's Little Africa, that area from Parnell Square back toward the North Circular Road, increasingly colonized by Africans, who had come to hitch a ride on the Celtic Tiger. He was also fairly at home in the food markets down near the river, where people knew him and where, in typical Dublin style, everybody called him "Judo." He enjoyed walking back from there each morning, the huge basket of fresh produce balanced skillfully on his head. He could sense people looking at him admiringly. Sometimes he would flash pearly teeth at some pretty girl, who would immediately turn pink. Then he would go home happy, dreaming impossible dreams.

But outside the little circle of Africans frequenting Shad's restaurant, the mostly friendly neighbors in adjoining streets, his market pals, and some clergy and faithful at the church where he worshipped, Jude knew virtually no one and was shy of making contact. In the six weeks he had spent in Dublin he had not encountered much racial hostility. Incoherent taunts in his back a few times, once a glutinous yellow snot landing at his feet, and another time, from a pretty girl on the arm of an ugly lout, obscene gestures, which sparked disgust and even pity in his heart, more than anger or fear.

But he had heard stories of what had happened to other people, those who had strayed from the African ghetto and dared to compete in other sectors of Irish society. He was in no hurry to do likewise. He knew nothing south of the river bisecting Dublin, not to mention anywhere outside the city. He had not even learned how to take a Dublin bus, use a public telephone, or handle any but the simplest commercial transactions. It was a slender basis for all that he had to do now.

Having dressed, Jude knelt down, as he always did.

"Sweet Jesus," he said, "my Savior, my brother, you are my only Shad now. You, too, are Nwachukwu, son of God. Make a home for Shad, break kola nut for him, heal his broken body, dry his tears, forgive his sins. Console our mother very well, and I will console your Mother. Help me, guide me everytime in what I must do. Make me worthy of my father, as you are worthy of your Father. Love me too much, I beg, I beg. Amen."

CHAPTER TWO

INSPECTOR JIM QUILLIGAN HAD NEVER HAD TO DEAL WITH Africans. They had only begun to appear in Ireland in numbers since the country had become prosperous, which was as recent as it was tenuous. Over the last five years they had been arriving in their thousands—though hardly so many as the Asians who, less conspicuous than the blacks, were by now inscrutably and charmingly present everywhere.

If Jude Okafor was anything to go by, Quilligan thought, he liked the blacks. There was fellow feeling, of course: Jude and he were both outsiders. Jude was an African and Jim was a tinker, an Irish gypsy. In terms of Irish society, there was not much to choose between the two.

A big man, whose ruddy complexion and yellow hair proclaimed his origins, Quilligan had traveled the roads of Ireland until his early teens, in a series of pony traps, campers, and beat-up motor cars. He had slept, eaten, washed, and performed all other natural functions in the open air, publicly or behind bushes and trees as appropriate. He had ridden wild piebald ponies bareback and at high speeds since before he could walk, and was always as healthy as a trout: he had even had to be tied to the backseat of a Land Rover for a week to prevent him bursting his belly open climbing trees in the aftermath of a nick-of-time appendectomy.

As a child, Quilligan had had no illusions about the *nice* people who lived in houses, or at least about their attitudes to the likes of himself. For most of them, he knew perfectly well, he was bottom of the pile: presumed to be lice-ridden, incontinent, an ex officio thief, trainee drunkard and splitter of skulls, very likely the bastard issue of incestuous coupling. He had learned humility early, but also pride, resilience, silence in the face of disdain, and never ever to be subservient. His self-image was intact, based on who he and his people were, and not on how the settled community might choose to regard them.

When Quilligan's father, wanting to give his children a better chance in life, and fearful for his wife's deteriorating health, had finally decided to settle down in a house, the change had been excruciating for all of them. They would remain for generations restless, not in the clawing, craving way of people cutting loose from dirty addictions, but in the nobler idiom of free spirits accustoming themselves to life in a cage. For years Jim had felt like a penguin that had once been an eagle.

Between a no-nonsense Christian Brothers school and Garda Training College at Templemore, Quilligan had learned to conform, externally at least. In head, heart, and intuition, however, he remained very much his own man. Superiors, always in dread of what he might do next, still valued his fearless honesty coupled with the shrewd insight and experience of one who had lived from his earliest days much closer to the harsher realities of life than any of them.

Quilligan was moved by Jude, by his incredible naïveté on the one hand, and his total determination on the other. Here was this boy, down from heaven in the last shower, an innocent abroad in a completely unfamiliar culture—and yet, gung ho to capture and kill his brother's murderer. He could not help smiling at the youngster's slogan: One and God is majority! There was no doubt in Jude's mind about who the "one" was, and even God himself, it seemed, would be getting no say about whose side He was meant to be on.

The first interview had not gone well. Quilligan arrived at the restaurant the morning after Jude had been brought by the police to identify his murdered brother. He sat with Jude and Margot in the empty dining room. Having confirmed that neither of them had the slightest idea about who might have wanted to see Shad dead, Quilligan asked about his mood and movements on the day he died. His mood, they said, had been cheerful, as it always was, and his movements predictable, at least until six o'clock on that evening.

"So what happened at six o'clock?"

"A telephone call. He came into the kitchen. Jude had gone out to get something; oil, I think," Margot said.

"Red pepper," Jude said.

"Whatever. Shad said he had to go out, and to keep things going until he came back. He went. He never did come back."

Quilligan looked at Jude.

"That's it. He never come again." He paused, then went on. "It was Monday night, not busy. We manage very fine. Done, finish by eleven o'clock. Madame Margot go home. I eat my food and go to bed."

"Weren't you worried?"

"Yes, now, I worry small. I hate when Shad is not here, like now I hate."

"Had he done this before?"

Jude paused, then answered with obvious reluctance.

"Not in work time . . . but sometimes after work."

"He would stay out all night?"

Jude looked at Margot. She nodded her head. He answered.

"Yes, sometime. He romance one lady."

"Who is she, this lady?"

The boy lifted his head defiantly. Margot answered quickly.

"A girl called Esther. He did not go there. I talked to her last night. She has not seen him for three weeks. She is terribly shocked."

"Is Esther a prostitute?"

There was total silence. Jude stood up abruptly and walked out of the room.

"He is upset, Inspector."

"Yes. But I need to know. Is she a prostitute?"

"Inspector, these boys have a hard life. They are lonely."

"Madame Margot, I am not here to improve anybody's morals, but there are things I need to know. A whole night with a prostitute costs money."

"Shad did not give Esther money; I am sure of that."

"Well, exactly: that may be the point! Prostitutes have pimps, and pimps don't like people mixing business with pleasure—at their expense. They punish people. Perhaps somebody was punishing Shad—and it just went too far."

Margot thought about that for a moment.

"Okay, yes, I can see what you mean. But I don't think it was like that. He wasn't there that night, or for weeks. But, anyhow if you really must know, her name is Esther Wilson. Henrietta Street, a few doors up from the pub, top floor."

"Wilson. White, is she?"

"She is black. Does it matter?" asked Margot.

"It could do. Racism. Did Shad have trouble that way?"

"Not really. The odd insult, not being welcome here or there, being treated like shit once or twice. We all get it. But Africa has grown big here. We are not afraid."

"Things were worse?"

"Good, then bad, now better. When we were small, nobody noticed. Now we are big, it is okay. In between, that was the bad time, when we were too big not to be trouble and too small to defend ourselves."

"Interesting. Tell me, had Shad anything wrong with his leg? He was hardly lining up for an operation, was he?"

"Of course not. He never went near doctors. All he ever had was fever now and again."

"Fever?"

"Malaria. We know how to handle that. Native cures."

"What about protection rackets, was he being pestered for protection money?"

"No, nothing like that, We look after each other around here. Besides, Shad didn't have money. Everyone knew that. Any he could spare he sent home to his mother for the young ones."

"A nice guy, huh?"

Her eyes moistened. "He was a prince among men," she said. Quilligan stood up.

"Where did Jude go?"

"The kitchen. That door." She pointed.

Jude was standing, looking out the window at nothing. There was nothing to look at except a blank wall. He did not turn around.

"What will you do now?"

"I will find my senior brother's murderer and kill him."

Quilligan smiled and shook his head.

"I mean about the restaurant."

"I will continue it, for Shad."

"Listen, Jude, I know this is all pain for you, but we are on the same side. We must help each other."

"I cannot bring money. I have no money. You are wasting your time, Inspector."

Quilligan went forward and put his hand on the boy's shoulder. There was no reaction.

"You probably won't believe this for a long time, but you will see in the end. I do not want money. What I *do* want is the same as you want, to catch whoever did this evil and cowardly thing."

Jude did not turn his head, but when Quilligan left moments later he heard very quietly behind him: *"Dalu."*

Margot opened the street door for him. He asked her:

"Why does Jude call you 'Madame Margot'?"

"Because that is what a well-mannered young man calls a senior lady in his country."

"I see. And what does *dalu* mean?"

"It means 'thank you.'"

The Murtaghs lived near the crest of soft hills known hyperbolically as the Dublin Mountains. Their house snuggled into a fold of the slope, a stone's throw below the ruined remains of the Hellfire Club, a notorious gambling haunt for the dandies, young bucks, and gay blades of eighteenth-century Dublin society. Inspector Quilligan and Sergeant Molly Power drove up there in the early afternoon.

The Murtaghs had a lot to say but little to add to what the police knew already: stormy night, security light woke them. No sound of a car. Jack *thinks* he heard a voice calling, presumably for help. When? Before or after the security light went on? Before or after Mary called him? He does not remember. When Mary first saw the black man, he was standing, presumably on one leg; he had to be, to ring the doorbell, but he collapsed as she watched him. They ran down, opened the door. No chitchat, only groans. He was hurting and bloody. A few telephone calls to doctors, hospitals. No joy. They dragged him into their car, nearly rupturing themselves and probably him in the process. He groaned and they groaned—a lot of groaning all 'round. They went inside, threw on some clothes, then drove him to the nearest hospital at Loughlinstown. Nightmarish stuff.

The Murtaghs' small garden, and the roadway for fifty yards on either side, had been cordoned off for several hours on the first day after Shad's death. When the forensic experts had done their thing, the road had been reopened to traffic and the cordon was repositioned to corral the Murtagh property and its roadside frontage for further examination. Quilligan had already had a preliminary report on his desk that morning. He walked the terrain now with Molly, report in hand.

The mountain road passed above the level of the Murtagh residence which, sheltered by hedges, was not visible from the roadway. Indeed, Quilligan had driven past it twice before he had spotted the entrance. Somebody unfamiliar with the place might well have thought it a deserted spot and a nice place to dump unwanted bodies.

There were fresh tire tracks coming from the city direction, then swerving across the narrow roadway and right in onto the grass margin fronting the Murtagh property. These tracks, which were made by 205mm tires in good condition, indicated that a large car had pulled over and stopped at that point. The right-hand front tire, though new, did have a notch on its inner rim, which printed quite plainly in the shallow mud at the roadside.

Flattened patches of grass and, farther in, of rougher under-growth, linked tenuously by minute particles of cloth, blood, and plastic, suggested that Shad had been dragged out of the car, then rolled about fifteen feet into a ditch where, it was no doubt hoped, he might lie undiscovered for ages or forever. Instead the body had apparently continued to roll out the other side of that ditch, which was shallow on the lower side, or Shad, when he came to, may even have been able to roll himself twenty yards farther downhill to a point from which he could crawl to the front door of the house. Molly, having lain down in the ditch herself, pointed out that the house, invisible from the roadside, could be seen *under* the hedge by somebody lying in that position. The dirty and torn condition of the victim's clothes and of the plastic bag enclosing his mutilated limb was consistent with this reconstruction.

"It could have worked," Molly said, as they drove back to the city, "but not a good place to hide a body, even if there was no house nearby. Much too near the road and no serious cover. Dogs, birds, anything could have drawn attention to it."

"So?" Quilligan prompted.

"So it was a rush job, one not expected to arise, and therefore not prepared for."

"Good. What else?"

"Probably done by one man."

"One *person,* let's say. Equal opportunity, after all."

"Or person then, who couldn't drag the body very far. Shad was not very big, but. . . ."

"All bodies are heavy. You are right," said Quilligan.

Molly, quite the contrary, felt strangely weightless as they descended into the breathtaking panorama of Dublin Bay, like space travelers floating back to earth in a returning space capsule. At the first traffic light, Quilligan said:

"Molly, expert surgery is the queer fish in this case. You and I have to queue two years for it: this guy gets a freebie when he doesn't even want it. What the hell is all that about?"

Molly put the same question to Jan-Hein that night in bed. They had discussed the case on and off since she got in from work that evening. Jan-Hein said, "How do you always get crazy cases? I mean, cutting someone's leg off must be the world's messiest way to murder someone. Are you sure it was a murder? Couldn't it be like an IRA thing, like a punishment beating or a knee-capping?"

"The IRA had nothing to do with this."

"No, of course not, but Al Qaeda or somebody. Don't the Muslims cut off things sometimes?"

"Don't be racist, Jan-Hein."

"No, seriously."

"Anyhow he wasn't a Muslim. I was with him when he died: I told you."

"Yes. You should tell his brother about that."

"Do you really think so?"

"I do; it would help him."

They dozed.

"Molly, suppose it was meant to be a murder, why then would they dump him in a ditch, when he was still alive? That was a sure sentence to death—but such a death. Do you know what he would have died of?"

"Loss of blood."

"No. Thirst. That is one lousy death: cut off a limb, and leave the guy to die of thirst. When you lose a lot of blood, you suffer agonies with thirst."

"So you think they *did* want to kill him—but slowly: they wanted to torture him to death?"

"Something like that."

"Holy Moses, hold me tight!"

"I'm not holy Moses, but I'll try!"

Later, Jan-Hein said:

"On the other hand . . ."

"What, you're not going to change it all again now, are you?"

"Well, it's just that people who torture other people to death like to watch them squirm. I mean, you don't just dump them in a hole and go home for tea."

"Oh my God, what kind of monster did I marry?"

"I'm just telling you the facts, ma'am, the facts."

Jude was carrying on with the business as best he could. He knew so much less about it than his brother had, but Margot was everywhere, early and late, advising, organizing, and, above all, doing. He had also taken on two boys to help, one Igbo, the other Yoruba. Both were enthusiastic and shaping up well. He needed whatever money he could earn. He was conscious, too, that many regular customers, single men, or at least men who had left wives and families behind them in Africa, were dependent on Shad's restaurant for their main meal at midday or in the evening. He must not disappoint them.

Inevitably, standards took a tumble. All festive or modestly exotic dishes disappeared from the menu overnight, and even the basic fare that continued to be served was sometimes less than satisfactory. But there was enormous sympathy for Jude. Not only were there no complaints, but people who had never given tips before, conscious of impending funeral expenses, suddenly became generous and even lavish. If on occasion Jude had to apologize for some culinary disaster, he was invariably met with that most Nigerian of reassurances: "Jude, you are trying."

Customers even began to help. If things were busy, they would get what they needed from the kitchen for themselves or for each other rather than hassle the hard-pressed and inexperienced staff. The ultimate in philanthrophic miracles was achieved two nights after Shad's death, when Fat Isaac, who claimed to be a great chief of Benue and to have three wives in Gboko, was discovered in the back kitchen helping mere women with the washing up.

Shad had died early on Wednesday morning. It was late Friday afternoon when the media got to hear of it. Within minutes the restaurant was chockablock with newshounds. Jude was alone with one of the new boys when they started to arrive. He was bombarded with questions, some of which he hardly understood, and most of which he did not know how to answer. He was asked about racism, tribal warfare, black magic, immigration rackets, and drug trafficking. He could only repeat again and again that Shad was a good man, who had no enemies and was involved in nothing illegal. About racism, he said that they had the best of neighbors and that he could not believe that any Dubliner or any Irish person would have done this thing to his brother.

"Well, who did it, Jude, who killed your brother?"

"I no know," he answered, dropping one open upturned palm into the other, in an eloquent African gesture of helpless bewilderment.

They wanted to know about Shad's love life. Jude laughed and said nothing. Unfortunately, it was this laughing image that several newspapers chose to publish next morning, leading to unfavorable commentaries among readers about Jude's attitude to his brother's death. But comedy and tragedy are half brothers, each being born of human fragility. So an African will sometimes laugh in the face of tragedy. This is neither callousness nor hysteria: it is simple acknowledgment of the human condition.

The reporters wanted a photograph of Shad. Jude had only the one in Shad's passport—the usual horrendous travesty—but he was not willing to part with it. The media eventually got the same photo from the police, who presumably had acquired it from the Immigration authorities.

By and large, the newspapers went with racism as the likely explanation for Shad's killing. Ordinary people everywhere were upset and ashamed and, over the following weeks, Jude received many messages of sympathy from total strangers, some including mass cards, presents, and even money toward funeral expenses.

Less welcome were the attentions of various radical groups who were keen to hijack Shad's story for their own purposes. Jude soon learned to avoid them. He was less on his guard against the professionals in moral indignation who ride into battle on the backs of the afflicted, always delighted with new and politically correct opportunites to spew anger and hatred.

To be buried in one's own village is important to every African. At first, Jude had been determined that Shad's body would be taken home for burial in the family compound. Friends, and especially elders of his people, had persuaded him that this was financially and logistically impossible. They had also assured him that he would not be failing in his duty if, like many immigrants before him, he had to settle for an Irish grave. An argument that helped was the example of numerous Irish reverend fathers and reverend sisters, missionaries who had died in Nigeria after decades of service, who had been happy, even eager, to sleep among *their people* in the red earth of Africa.

Besides, Jude had to admit that his uncles, who ruled the family, would probably not approve of repatriation nor allow Shad to be buried in the family compound. One traditional viewpoint was that to die so young, in such a way, and unmarried, was, in some measure, a disgrace, even a sign of the ancestors' displeasure. If it had happened at home, Shad would probably have been buried hurriedly in the bush, the very same evening, and not in the compound, which is reserved for married elders.

Sadly, Jude accepted that when the police released the body—promised for the following Wednesday after the autopsy—Shad would be buried in Glasnevin Cemetry. The Vincentian Fathers at St. Peter's Church, Phibsborough, had promised a full-blown African vigil, a solemn Mass and burial, and the whole African community was committed to preparing a funeral service and a subsequent "entertainment" worthy of an emir or an *oba*.

CHAPTER THREE

INSPECTOR QUILLIGAN WAS NOT BEING GRATUITOUSLY OF-fensive when he had asked if Esther Wilson was a prostitute. He needed to know. Three years previously, a notorious inner-city pimp had been returned to his maker with a slender poisoned arrow lodged between his shoulder blades. A cruel and greedy man, he had been sadistically vicious with a black girl who had been looking after black boys and didn't see why she couldn't keep the few euros they had been able to pay her.

The police presumed that the black boys, in retaliation, had arranged for this exotic departure, poisoned arrows being more in the tropical tradition than in the local idiom. The black boys were asked about it. They replied with impressive unanimity, and with much dropping of one open upturned hand into the other upturned open hand, that only a Fulani warrior would know how to make a poisoned arrow, and that, as there were no Fulani warriors in Dublin at that precise moment in history, how the poor gentleman had managed to get killed by a poisoned arrow was a fundamentally insoluble problem. The police were not happy with this answer, but their inquiries got no further.

Meanwhile, as there is fairly widespread respect internationally for poisoned arrows, Dublin pimps became circumspect in their dealings with African women.

Quilligan checked with the vice squad. Esther Wilson was not a prostitute, he was told, at least not in the sense of walking a beat or soliciting publicly. She was a shop assistant, who devoted leisure moments to men, mostly black, who called at her top-floor apartment. Pimps and police knew about her. So far, neither had interfered with her unusual social service. Tom McMahon of the vice squad did not think that Shad's death was the opening shot in renewed warfare between pimps and prostitutes.

"Amputations and ether, Jim, that's not the Dublin vice scene!"

"Neither was poisoned arrows, Tom. Still it happened."

"A once-off, Jim. One swallow don't make a summer. Besides, your boy was only marginal. In every sense an amateur—God be good to him! Nations don't go to war over the likes of him."

Esther Wilson was an attractive woman, black by birth, red-haired by chemical arrangement, all curves. Probably in her forties, she looked thirty. Daughter of a Dublin prostitute and a long-departed African diplomat, she cultivated friendships, as she emphatically called them, among the male African population of the city. She agreed forcefully with Inspector McMahon: she was not a prostitute.

"I have many friends, Inspector, that is all. Shad was a very close friend."

"Do your close friends give you money?"

"Shad never gave me money. It was not like that."

"He loved you, is that it?"

"I can't say that he loved me: I certainly loved him. He was a nice boy."

"So I'm told."

"Believe it. Listen, Inspector, Shad came here when he couldn't help himself. Can you understand that?"

"Yes." He looked at her and he could.

"I wonder. Anyhow, since his kid brother arrived he tried to cut down on his visits."

"Good example for the little missionary boy, huh?"

She smiled ironically.

"Something like that, Inspector. You are so understanding. I haven't seen Shad six times in the last six months—I mean here in my flat. I've seen him at Mass, all right, and around town. But, after Jude came, as you say, he wanted to be a good boy again. You remember how that goes, do you?"

"Oh yes. Was Shad here the night he died?"

She shook her head slowly and sadly.

"I wish he had been, Inspector, I wish it with all my heart. He would still be alive if he had. But no, he was not here. Strange, isn't it? That's what you get for being a good boy."

"Have you any idea . . . ?"

"No, Inspector. Save your breath. I have no idea where he was, or who could have killed him."

"Enemies?"

"Poor Shad. You couldn't be his enemy, not if you tried."

"The media say it is racism."

"The media, the media, what the hell do the media know about it?"

Familiar roles: Quilligan was saying what he did and did not think. Molly Power was doing the devil's advocate.

"A black man who everybody loves gets mutilated and murdered, for no possible reason: that has got to be racism," Molly insisted.

"Look, the country is full of idiots, agreed, airheads who spit and shout 'nigger,' schoolyard bullies who never grew up. Then, at another level, loads of people are snobs. They think that anyone different is inferior, and has no right to be here—except, of course, to clean up their muck and empty the dust bins. All right, they are all racists, if you like. But there is one hell of a difference between that sort of small-minded prejudice and cold-blooded murder."

"Well, as you never tire of telling me, if the wind is in the right quarter, if you get the right mix, or the wrong chemistry, even nice people can commit murder."

"Yes, but what's the mix, or the wind, or the chemistry here? Nothing, Molly. This isn't something that happened at a pop concert or a football match or in some sleazy bar at three o'clock in the morning. There is no context here of hate or sudden anger, of lashing out in drunken fury.

"I mean, even suppose that this was done by the worst kind of racist sadist, by somebody who wanted to torture and terrify, what in God's name is an anesthetic doing in there in the middle of it? That is the maverick element in this case. It makes garbage of all the reasonable explanations."

"So then what do we do, Jim, in practice?"

"I'll tell you what we do, Molly, in practice. To please the media and our sensitive-souled superiors, who want the media off their backs ASAP, we will waste the next week pulling in the lunatic fringe of right-wing politics and a whole army of total airheads with pink hair and walrus tusks stuck through their nipples, their navels, and their nostrils. That's Dublin's official racists."

"Sounds like fun."

"You have got to be joking. This is where I come closest to punching somebody. These people are just so arrogant and so stupid, they can't even sit upright on a chair. I'd prefer to be questioning orangutans in the zoo."

Molly laughed.

"Now, who is being racist?"

"Guilty—and not sorry!"

On Sunday afternoon, Jude was lying on a wooden bench in the empty restaurant having siesta. Somebody rapped at the street door, which was locked. He swung his feet to the ground and, with shirt hanging out and zip half down, tottered to the door.

She was slightly older than himself, smaller, and so beautiful, he thought, that he gasped. He had never been so close to any white girl before, and certainly not to one like this: eyes so blue, like pools of deep water, soft translucent skin, silken shoulder-length hair, not red nor brown, not blonde, some magic in-between color he could not name, firm breasts like well-rounded coconuts, only inches from his beating heart. Electricity coursed down his spine, while in front he fumbled to arrange his clothes more decently.

"Excuse me disturbing you. Are you Mr. Okafor?"

He had to think about that. Nobody had ever called him "mister."

"I'm Jude."

"Oh yes, You are so like your brother."

"Did you know Shad?"

She half opened her lips, hesitated, then answered.

"I was with him when he died."

Jude stood back, opening the door wide.

"Please come in, I beg."

He closed the door behind her and led the way to the corner table where he had sat with Margot and the policeman.

"Can I bring you food, a soft drink, anything?"

"No, thank you. Will you sit down? Can I talk to you?"

He sat opposite her.

"Tell me about Shad, I beg, tell me everything," he said.

He stretched strong fine-boned hands across the table, entreating her.

"That is why I came. I thought, if it was my brother, I would like to know."

"Oh thank you. You are a nurse, a doctor perhaps?"

"No, I am a policewoman."

"Oh!"

"Does that make a difference?"

He hesitated, then said:

"Why were you there? What were you doing?"

"When the doctor saw that your brother had been attacked, and that he was dying—because I'm afraid he was—well, a crime had clearly been committed, so they sent for the police. I happened to be in the nearest patrol car, so I went there. I hoped that Shad might be able to tell me something. . . . Well, sadly, he wasn't."

"Was he suffering?"

"When they brought him in, yes, I suppose he was in pain. But they had given him an injection, or whatever they do; he was comfortable . . . and he was very brave."

"Thank Jesus!"

"They had given him blood transfusions, too, but they knew it was too late. He was on a trolley. They wheeled him into a little

annex. That is just a little private space where they can put people . . ."

"To die," Jude said.

"I suppose so, Jude."

"Did he say something?"

"His name, 'Shad.' The others went away. I stayed with
him . . . until the end. I held his hand, and said some prayers. I
think he liked that. He looked at me all the time. Two or three
times he said something, just a word. He would say it once. Then
he would say it again in a few moments. It sounded like 'nay.' He
would say it very softly."

Jude bent his head. His shoulders trembled.

"What does it mean?" she asked gently.

"It is *Nne*. It is what an Igbo child calls his mother."

He lifted his head and smiled through tears. Such a beautiful
face, she thought: eyes like she had never seen in a boy before,
enormous, wide, dark brown in dazzling white, between long
black lashes that any girl would die for.

"There was something else."

"Tell me."

"Before he died, about ten minutes before, he became agitated."

"Please, what is 'agitated'?"

"Agitated means restless. He was searching at his neck, at his
collar, as if looking for something. He was feeling at his throat
and across his chest. Like this."

She demonstrated, fingers coaxing her own sweet throat and
breasts. Jude noticed and nodded.

"I asked him: 'Shad, what are you looking for?'"

"I can guess," Jude said.

"He said, 'chaplet, chaplet.' Then he suddenly took my wrist in both his hands. I was wearing a bracelet of garnets, you know, semiprecious stones. We are not meant to wear jewelry when we are in uniform, but anyhow, I was wearing that bracelet. Shad took it between his fingers and held it quietly until he died, a few minutes later. I don't know what he meant."

Jude nodded his head again gently.

"I do know. He was looking for his chaplet. He always wore that one around his neck, day and night, like I do."

He undid his top shirt buttons to show a rosary of bottle-green glass beads circling his neck, the crucifix nestling in the light hairs of his chest.

Lucky Jesus! Molly thought. "That is lovely," she said.

"Me and Shad, we like this chaplet very well. Pope John Paul was coming to Onitsha years ago, to make saint of Reverend Father Tansi. I follow Shad that day. We see the pope. It was too hot. The people is all dying of thirst. We make too much money selling water to all the people that day. God is mighty! We earn plenty money. Then we go buy this special chaplets—see, here is Father Tansi face on this side of the little medal, and here is pope's face. Then the Holy Father, he bless us all and all our chaplets. Then we bring chaplets home for all our junior ones. We never take that chaplet off again, except for pray it and bath. Are you sure Shad's was vanish?"

"Well, I saw no sign of it. He obviously thought my bracelet was a rosary. It made him happy at the end. He died very peacefully. That is really what I wanted to tell you."

Jude stood up and came around the table. He knelt on one knee, like a knight to his dubbing. Taking her hands in his, he kissed each of them solemnly.

"I thank you with all my heart. Praise God!"

CHAPTER FOUR

JIM QUILLIGAN AND JUDE SHARED AN UNSPOKEN CONVICtion that nothing would happen about finding the murderer until after the funeral. In Jude's case, this was a conscious decision, or rather a clear recognition that his first duty was to prepare spiritually and materially for the most moving and splendid thanksgiving and burial service he could possibly arrange for his brother. He had no idea how he would pay for it, yet he felt that this was the easiest of the impossible tasks laid on his shoulders. God would provide for the funeral.

Would God, the God of Jesus Christ who forgave sinners, would *that* God still be with him, once Shad had been decently laid to rest? Because then he, Jude Ekemauche, urged on by the spirit and blood of his ancestors, by the tradition and pride of his people and tribe, would give his whole self, body and soul, to the hunt for Shad's killer. By God's grace, he hoped with all his heart, he would find that person and kill him with his own hands.

For Quilligan the issues were less dramatic. He was well familiar with this totally unrewarding phase in practically every investigation. This was the time for spreading the net patiently and catching nothing, for foot slogging, for routine inquiries, and for false trails that led nowhere but had to be followed, if only to be able to say that this or that suspect had been checked out and eliminated from the inquiry. This was all the more tedious in the present case, as there were no plausible suspects in sight, only stereotyped categories of suspect: skin-headed zombies, right-wing fanatics, sadists, lager louts banned from every football ground in Europe. Even as vague groups of suspects, they all lacked credibility as Shad's killers, because of the same awkward, out-of-place sticking point in every case: the anesthetic.

Quilligan had received preliminary reports from the autopsy team. The anesthetic administered, they told him, had been more than a simple knock-out pill. One of these had indeed been used as a preliminary, most likely served up in a drink, as currently favored by date rapists. But Shad, once rendered unconscious, had been seriously anesthetized and kept under for at least two hours. If the surgery performed during that time had been at least competent, and the postoperative patching up rudimentary but adequate, the use of anesthetics could only be described as reckless and way below any acceptable standard. Approximate and badly monitored, in an area requiring absolute precision, this anesthetic had caused severe respiratory problems that could have killed an older or less fit person than Shad, even without the added factors of blood loss and shock.

Quilligan called at the restaurant at lunchtime on the following Tuesday. He had some good news to tell Jude, and he was glad of the pretext to sit in the dining room sizing up the clientele and absorbing the atmosphere. This was why he had come at a time when he knew that Jude would be too busy to sit down immediately and talk. Wedged against a tiny table near the door, the inspector ordered what he thought he saw at the next table—yellow-buttered mashed potatoes and lamb in parsley sauce—and began to look inconspicuously, as he again thought, about him.

His meal arrived promptly, served with extravagant wrist flourishes by one of Jude's smiling acolytes. It came heavily garnished in culture shock. The "lamb" was wolf in sheep's clothing, as were the potatoes in their own vegetal way. To the discerning palate, there is nothing wrong with *cassava*-and-goat-in-*egusi* soup—but Quilligan's palate had been educationally disadvantaged by the itinerant lifestyle of his early years. Savoring *cassava* and goat was not among his acquired skills.

Not wishing to cause offense, he tried manfully to eat a few mouthfuls of either *cassava* or goat. He soon realized that, even for the sake of world peace, this was not an option. He then spent five deceitful minutes redeploying the food around his plate in such a way as to suggest serious inroads. To no avail. Flattered by the white man's interest in Igbo cuisine, the kitchen had assigned him a particularly ample portion which, no matter how he remarshaled it, always ended up as critical mass in some area of his plate. Meanwhile the glutinous *egusi* soup, excited by his efforts to make the *cassava* disappear, was oozing horribly onto the table from all 360 degrees of his plate's circumference.

Ireland's difficulty was Africa's opportunity. A sharp-eyed boy-child alighted from nowhere on the chair opposite Quilligan, smiling winningly and rubbing his palms up and down together, which in African sign language denotes willingness to relieve somebody of something. Never was charity more blessed in the giving than in the taking. Quilligan had his plate back within minutes, shining clean, and everybody in the room burst into good-natured laughter. Without seeming to, they had all been watching the watcher.

A fat mama in a floor-length robe and matching turban arose at the farthest end of the room and came, half dancing, half shuffling, toward him across the floor.

"Praise the Lord!" she intoned, waving her arms in what could have been a championship swimming stroke.

"Amen!" replied heartily all present, except Quilligan.

"Praise the Lord, brother!" she insisted, personalizing it this time, and upping the decibels considerably.

"A-men!" repeated his commensals, who were now standing and clapping to the rhythm of the fat lady's dance.

"Praise the Lord Almighty, because this poor chil' be orphan *pickin* and the good Lord feed am everytime!"

The designated orphan *pickin*, hugely pleased with himself and the Lord, and the attention that they were jointly getting, grinned from ear to ear and was gone.

Shortly afterward, Jude brought Quilligan into the kitchen and sat him at a table where Margot put an alternative plate of food before him. Pounded yam and some deliciously succulent meat, which looked and tasted like steak tartare. After a while Jude came and sat beside him. Quilligan was happy to find him more friendly and relaxed than at their first meeting.

"Jude, I have some good news to tell you, for a change."

"Oh yes? Tell me that one."

"I had a call this morning from Patrick Finnerty. He is one of Dublin's biggest undertakers. He asked me to give you a message."

"What is 'undertaker'?"

"An undertaker is the person who does funerals, you know, supplies coffins, big cars, arranges for the grave, so on and so forth."

"What is coffin?"

Margot explained.

"Coffin is casket."

"Anyhow, Mr. Finnerty says that he is very sad about what has happened to Shad . . . and to you. He is offering you his services for free. He will pay for everything."

Margot explained this to Jude in detail. He shook his head in amazement. His reply, when he found his voice eventually, might not have pleased Mr. Finnerty entirely. He said simply:

"God is mighty!"

When Quilligan was about to go, he asked on an impulse, "What was that beautiful meat, Jude? It was delicious."

"Dog."

"Dog!" exclaimed Quilligan, almost retching.

"Yes, best Irish terrier."

This time he did retch.

"I am joking." Jude laughed. "Some tribes do eat dog: we don't serve it here."

"Thanks be to God. So what was it?"

"Snake."

Quilligan retched again and fumbled for his handkerchief.

"Yes, puff adder. Very top quality food! Shad keep this one for pregnant woman."

"Why?" Quilligan gasped.

"Puff adder have very terrible bite. He make you bleed very plenty inside. All your guts go bleed. You go die now. Finish!"

Quilligan, by now beyond mere retching, was feeling quite unwell.

"But puff adder very lazy fellow. You annoy him very plenty before he bite. You even stand on him, he no bite—unless you stand on him for tail. He sleep everytime. So you give this one to pregnant woman. Her *pickin* go sleep everytime; he never go kick her for belly inside."

Madame Margot was very happy to hear about Finnerty's offer. "Jude, that is terrific.

When you add it all up, he is giving you anything between five and ten thousand euro. Where would you have got that kind of money?"

"Praise God!"

He paused, obviously thinking, then he asked his question.

"Madame Margot, why is Mr. Finnerty doing this, and why did he send the police to say it?"

"The police? I suppose it was the easiest way. He probably told his office to arrange it, and that is how they did it. The whites are like that, you know. They are scared of emotions. If Mr. Finnerty came here himself, and we started to cry, he would not know what to do. It would be as if we took our clothes off in front of his nose."

Jude laughed.

"I am not crying this time: I am laughing. It is very plenty money. So why did he do it?"

"Well, he is probably ashamed of what happened to Shad. A lot of Irish people feel guilty about it. But there is another reason."

"Yes?"

"Yes, Mrs. Finnerty, his wife. She is an artist. Shad used to model for her sometimes."

"Model?"

"Yes, he let her paint him."

"What? You mean without his clothes on!"

Margot laughed sadly.

"Ah Lordy me, how protective you are for each other! No, Jude, nothing like that. They were usually studies for religious pictures, black saints, that sort of thing: St. Martin de Porres, St. Maurice, Benedict the Black, Black Moses. As for clothes, I suppose he took off or put on whatever was necessary for the picture she was painting."

"But why Shad? Why was he with these people?"

"I cannot remember how they first met. I think Mrs. Finnerty just saw him somewhere and said he was just right for what she wanted. Shad was a nice-looking man, Jude."

"I know."

"Besides, he earned some extra money doing that, and he needed the money. Shad always said that Mrs. Finnerty was a very nice woman. I am sure she is the one who got her husband to do this about the funeral."

"I never even heard of half those saints. Were they all black?"

"So Shad said. Mrs. Finnerty had some books, he said, that gave all the paintings in the world that have ever been made of black people, including those saints. That is where she got her ideas. The only one I ever saw was a Christmas crib picture she did, with Shad as one of the Three Kings bringing gifts to Baby Jesus: gold, frankincense, and myrrh. Shad was the black king, of course. He looked wonderful: every inch a king, with gorgeous robes and jewels, and a gold crown on his head. We must find out where that picture is."

"Shad was carrying the myrrh, wasn't he?"

"I don't know, Jude, I can't remember."

"It had to be. The myrrh was to anoint Jesus' body for his burial, wasn't it?"

"Was it, Jude? I don't know."

He nodded slowly three times.

When Quilligan got home that evening he kissed his wife and said, "I've got news for you."

"Oh, what's that?"

"I've been eating snake. I think I'm pregnant."

Shad's wake was in the best African tradition. Contrary to all diocesan and parochial practice, St. Peter's Church remained open all night. Every black person in Dublin seemed to be there: Christians of all denominations, Muslims, and others who marched to still older drums. There were many white people, too, neighbors, traders, reverend sisters, many of them returned missionaries, and the ordinary people of the inner city who, instinctively, in the familiar bond of death, recognized Shad as one of their own, a true Dub.

All night long they kept their brother company, with songs and prayers, with drums, *gong-gong*, and kora. They recited rosary after rosary. From time to time, as the spirit moved them, people stood at the ambo and spoke, people young and old, educated and unlearned. They spoke of Our Savior's sufferings, and of Shad's, of God's sweet love and forgiveness, of the happiness of heaven, and of how we must thank God "everytime," because "he loves us too much." During that entire night, not one angry or vengeful word was spoken.

To Jude's great joy, two cousins had come from England, which meant that the family was represented in some way. Throughout the night vigil he remained absorbed in his own feelings and prayers, and yet acutely aware of every smallest detail. He could feel Shad very near him, and other powerful and protective presences, single and multiple, named, unnamed, and beyond all naming.

When morning came, there was the Mass, celebrated as the triumph of life over death. No Dublin church had ever seen or heard anything quite like it.

It was time to close the coffin. Jude stood beside his brother for the last time. The embalmers had done their best. "Shad, Shad," he whispered, "you smell like white man! Never mind. You look shiny. Your suit is standard. And thank you, Shad. *Dalu, O dalu.* Go well, my darling brother, go well. May Jesus give you perfect rest. May Mary bring you safely home."

He took his most precious possession, the green glass rosary beads, from around his neck and twined it between his brother's fingers. Then he turned and walked away quickly from the coffin, hands to his face, the tears bursting between his fingers and running down his wrists into his shirtsleeves.

After the mass, there were the crowds outside the church, handshakes, hugs, even kisses from complete strangers. Black people had already consoled him in the days since Shad's death. They had said "sorryo!" or Igbo words and short phrases that said everything:

Ewo-o! Chineke-e! Chukwu me'bere! He had embraced them, said thank you, *dalu,* or just said nothing. Sometimes he had cried and exclaimed, *Anwumo-o!* Then whoever was near had held him very tight.

Now people were saying long complicated things to him in English, holding onto his hand as if they had forgotten to give it back. When Shad's name was uttered, it sounded like a nick-name, not a real name or a real person. Most people did not men-tion Shad at all and seemed to want to tell Jude instead how devastated *they* felt. This puzzled him. What were they expect-ing? Was he meant to start consoling *them?* At one point he caught himself thinking how much better it would be if *he* had died and Shad was there coping with all these people. Shad would know what to say: he did not.

Meanwhile other people kept telling him things: that this was the archbishop and that was the minister for something or other, and those were the local TDs. What were TDs, he wondered. Still others were the chairpersons, presidents, or representatives of organizations he had never heard of. There was somebody im-portant looking from the Nigerian Embassy who, he thought, must be annoyed to have to put down his whole morning doing this.

He had no idea what to say to all these dignitaries, who at least did not tell him about how *devastated* they felt. They projected in-stead an aura of being weighed down still further by the burdens placed on their important shoulders by Shad's importunate de-parture. Perhaps he should apologize?

On the positive side, Jude was pleased with Shad's casket. It was of solid wood and had fancy silk linings. At home most peo-ple were buried in thick papier-mâché caskets. The limousines, too, were "standard:" long, black, sleek, and very clean. He and his cousins, Margot, Esther, the elders, Fat Isaac—not exactly in-vited but considering it his due—the restaurant staff, and the or-phan *pickin*—who got to share everything—and others whom he simply did not know, all crammed into the two cars and traveled in state to and/or from Glasnevin Cemetery.

The cemetery was another matter. It horrified him. Surreal,

unlike anything he had ever seen, it made him nauseous and dizzy. Hemmed in on all sides by hundreds of cement and stone rectangles, with their pygmy private gardens and ill-assorted monuments, he felt trapped and disoriented. The rows upon rows of burial plots seemed to him like a vast, ominously orderly, European-style traffic jam. It was as if, at any moment, a light up ahead would go green and the graves would surge forward, plunging, wave after wave of them, over a cliff and into the sea. It reminded him of the gospel story about the pigs on a mountainside that did just that. He felt so guilty to be abandoning Shad in such a place.

Shad will hate it, he thought miserably; he will understand that I was too ignorant to do better, but he will hate it. Some day, I will bring you home, Shad, if it is the last thing I do. I promise by God's grace and by all the spirits of our people.

The "entertainment" was, in Jude's own words, "very decent." The celebrating mourners proliferated through every nook and corner of the restaurant and its meager living quarters, then spilled out onto the sidewalk, along the street, and into the ground floor of buildings to left and to right. One of these was an African barber's, another a snooker hall where the Yoruba owner, having covered his precious tables as best he could against spoil and spillage, yielded up his space to eating and drinking: activities which were never, ever allowed there in normal times.

There was palm wine, mature and potent, and even *kiki* for the elders, soft drinks in great economy bottles for the unmarried and for women, and beer for fathers of families, especially Guinness, as black beer is undoubtedly good for black men—provided, of course, that they are married. In traditional African society, unmarried young men who smoke or drink alcohol are regarded as bad characters, in danger of ending up as armed robbers, cheats, or in politics.

Such food was never seen before or since: pounded yam, *jollof* rice, chicken, roast corn, strips of smoked and barbecued fish, meat done Hausa style and "too delicious," and wonderful *mie-mie*, a purée of beans prepared by the most skillful of the women. The best African eating house in town—after Shad's Place, of course—sent up several great platters of food from their base in Moore Street, including soups, bitter-leaf, *okoro, ogbonor, edikaiko.*

That evening, Jude was resting, stretched out on a bench in the deserted dining room, while Margot, indefatigable, bustled around finding things to do.

They chatted happily about the day, knowing that Shad had been given a wonderful send-off. He and all who loved him would be so proud. Suddenly Margot said:

"Jude, you lost your rosary beads, the Blessed Cyprian Tansi one."

"I didn't lose it. I gave it to Shad."

"When?"

"I put it in his hands before they closed his casket. He had lost his own."

"Well, whose are these then?"

Jude raised his head quickly. Margot was holding green glass rosary beads, unmistakably, a Father Tansi chaplet.

"Where did you get that?" he asked.

He held out his hand and took it.

"It was in one of the funeral cars. When we got back here after the burial, I was missing my purse. In fact, I had left it in the kitchen, but I thought I had lost it, so I went back to the cars to search. I didn't know which car I had been in; they are both exactly the same. So I searched both cars. I found the rosary beads in the second car. It was under the seat, as well as so many other things—a two-euro coin, a Biro, a comb—it is amazing what you find under car seats."

"Well, it cannot be my rosary beads: I gave mine to Shad. I wonder who owns this one? Other people may have them, too, of course. There must have been twenty people in and out of those two cars, some going to the cemetery, some coming back."

"Jude, I never saw anybody else with those beads. They were very special."

"Unless . . . unless somebody took my beads back from Shad, then dropped them in the car. You know we often showed our beads to people. They were very special, you are right about that. Somebody could *jealous* them. And I wasn't there when they put on the lid . . . I couldn't bear it . . . I was pouring out tears. I ran away like a small boy. Someone could have thieved them then, when my back was turned."

"But Jude, would somebody steal them from the hands of a dead man? That would bring very bad luck."

"Some people think it bring plenty good luck—like a relic. In old times people would take everything from a holy person when he go die. They even cut off parts from his body . . ."

There was a shocked silence when they both realized what he had just said. Jude let his head fall back heavily on the bench and closed his eyes. Margot went back to her work.

CHAPTER FIVE

By the middle of April Jim Quilligan knew scientif-ically what he had known intuitively for several weeks: his inquiry was going nowhere. With the help of Sergeant Molly Power, he had interviewed a disconcertingly large number of people, mostly men, but including also some women, who were known to the Gardaí as militantly and offensively anti-immigrant. The police were not concerned with people who, for economic, social, or even religious reasons, believed that Irish jobs, Irish morals, or even the whole Irish way of life—whatever that may be—were at risk from the increasing flow of immigrants from Africa, Asia, and Eastern Europe. Small-minded and alarmist such people might be, they were still entitled to their opinions. So long as their tactics remained within the limits of safety and public order, the police had no quarrel with them.

Quilligan was targeting a smaller hard-core group of fanatics who obsessively and publicly detested immigrants, and especially people of color, and who were known to be prepared to use in-timidation and hate tactics to impose their views. Some of these were mad, most of them plain bad, and all of them depressingly ignorant. In the hope of dredging up some useful information,

Quilligan and Molly had sat for hours listening to an endless flow of racist rants, both from people who seemed otherwise intelligent and from others who were patently morons.

They were told that blacks are missing a chromosome, that they represent a primitive stage of evolution and are destined to disappear. All blacks are oversexed, they were warned—with more than a hint of envy—and totally irresponsible. So they will soon be wiped out by AIDS and venereal diseases. Sour grapes! Quilligan thought to himself, knowing from experience that censoriousness usually flows from disappointment. Meanwhile, in flat contradiction with the dire prophecies of imminent annihilation, it was repeatedly asserted that black women in great numbers are getting pregnant and rushing to Dublin to have their babies, as part of a concerted strategy of colonization by reproduction. If this kind of ignorant thinking could lead to major changes in the laws and constitution of the country—as it had—it might also lead to an occasional mindless murder.

As well as all that promiscuity and propagating, the blacks, he was told, are busy being greedy, lazy, corrupt, dishonest, childish, and irredeemably tribal. They are incapable of governing themselves or of absorbing and implementing the sophisticated principles of modern administration and law making. In the same breath, and with crude inconsistency, it was added that Africans, and especially Nigerians, are devilishly clever at every sort of abstruse scam, excelling in banking, computer, and credit-card fraud.

Quilligan knew only too well from personal experience what it means to be at the receiving end of contempt and prejudice, simply for belonging to a particular race or group. It took all of his long apprenticeship in patience not to get sucked into flaming rows with these arrogant bully boys. Instead he kept his mind focused on the one relevant question: In all of this septic invective, was there the slightest scintilla of evidence that any one or number in this ugly procession of people haters had murdered Shad Okafor? Almost unfortunately, he concluded, the answer had to be no. They were nasty cretins—no doubt about that—but they were not murderers.

There had been other inquiries, of course: the autopsy and the technical examination of Shad's clothes and of the terrain at the Murtagh residence. The usual flotsam and jetsam had been picked up: hairs, scraps of fabric, clay, food, dried body fluids—mucus and sweat, dust, traces of a deodorant or aftershave lotion—something masculine anyhow, and even some DNA which was not Shad's. These items could reflect places he had been and people he had interacted with. They could be valuable eventually, if the police got to having suspect persons and places to try them against for size.

Molly checked on the telephone call Shad received that night shortly before he left the restaurant to go and get murdered. If it was a land line call, it would be recorded for billing. Cellphone calls, impossible to trace, except by triangulation during transmission, can also be traced through billing—unless it is one of those money-up-front phones. In either case, it helps to know whose bill you should be looking at. If the call was made from a public coinbox, it might be traced back to where it was made from, but who knows whose hand had held the handset?

The technician Molly had to talk to about the telephone call clearly fancied himself at the cutting edge of rocket science. He also enjoyed talking down to a woman and was visibly torn between the desire to show off how much he knew and the pleasure of remaining impenetrably incomprehensible. When asked, finally, to do his best to trace that call, he sighed heavily, like a golfer being put upon to do a hole-in-one from a tee in Phoenix Park to a sloping green on the planet Mars. That he possessed the required trigonometry was not to be doubted. An accumulation of more weighty responsibilities was understood to be the only problem.

The police had been in no hurry to confront the African community directly, feeling that the preliminaries were best left to the Africans themselves. All their contacts with these people, from the time of Shad's death through to the funeral, which both Molly and Quilligan had attended, had left them in no doubt about the affection and respect for Shad within the black community and the groundswell of sympathy and support for his brother. There would be no cover-up, no conspiracy of silence, no sly taking of sides with a murderer against Shad and Jude. The best police strategy was to hold back and wait for what, given time, should rise spontaneously to the surface. Molly said:

"If they know anything, Jim, or even suspect anything—they may not tell us, but they will not hide it from Jude, or at least from some authority figure, some elder within their own community."

"That's right. I remember how it was among my own people, the tinkers. You'd never tell 'the Guards' anything, or even open your beak if they were sniffing around. But once they backed off, then yes, people would talk among themselves—and reach conclusions—and even punish somebody who needed to be punished."

"Punish, like how?"

"Hell, you're the *Guards*, I can't tell you that!"

He winked at her, and went on:

"What I will tell you is that young Jude is just like what I would have been at his age. He has every intention of killing Shad's killer if he can get to him one minute before we do. He as good as told me so."

"And will he get there before we do?"

"Well, the dice is loaded against him, isn't it? He barely knows the name of this bloody country, let alone how to move around in it. But he still could do it, yes. He is intelligent, he is totally committed, and he has—what is it? Character, charisma, the X factor. Besides, he has his ear to the ground in a way that we couldn't possibly have."

"So perhaps it is time for us to move in on his turf. That's where the action is, in Little Africa. If anyone in there knows something, it has surely come to the surface by now."

"Right, missus! Let's get in there tomorrow and listen. It will be a nice change from talking to those other morons."

Tunde, the Yoruba snooker hall owner who had lent his premises for the postburial entertainment, now put a small room at police disposal. Here Quilligan and Molly Power took it in turns to talk with members of the black community. The word had been put out that they were okay, and people, eager to see Shad's murderer brought to justice, came willingly to explore with them whether anything they knew, or might have heard or seen could help toward solving the crime.

The Yoruba man himself was first off the blocks. As Shad's next-door neighbor and the leisure time provider for many of the restaurant's patrons, he was well informed about what people were thinking and saying, and what, if anything, they knew about Shad's murder. What he had to say confirmed everything that the police had seen for themselves. Shad—and Margot, to whose goodness he had given free rein—were highly regarded. The restaurant was a focal point for the African community. More than just somewhere to eat, it was a place to find friends, support, and courage, especially when the going was rough. The case of Pita, the orphan *pickin,* was mentioned with approval and pride by several people. As one dancing mama phrased it:

"This chil' never go one time for sleep on empty stomach."

The Yoruba made one frank and revealing admission:

"Most the shops and business around this place belong to Yoruba man and thick madam."

"Thick madam?" asked Molly, intrigued by the graphically physical image. "Do you mean a fat lady?"

The Yoruba laughed uproariously.

"Well, sometimes they are—how do you say?—well upholsteried. But no, 'thick madam' means one big business lady. What I am saying is that the Yorubas control most of the business around this place. So when one Igbo boy come park his load onto our compound, tell the truth, we are not very delighted."

"You mean Shad was not welcome here."

"First time around, he was not welcome, no. You see, Yorubas and Igbos do not always like themselves very well. Yoruba, one big tribe west of Niger; Igbo, one big tribe east of Niger. The Igbos go find oil on their side. Then they make their own country. 'Biafra' they call this one, and they no go share this oil with Yoruba. So we have civil war."

"Wasn't that war something about the Igbos being persecuted because they were Christians?"

"That is how Igbo man tells the story. It is true, Igbo Catholic worry with Hausa Muslim in the North, but not with Yoruba man in the West. They say that we betray them in the war by not coming on their side against the Hausa. I think that, next time around, it will be different. Think of Chief Abiola!"

Already lost in the complexities of Nigerian politics, Molly headed back for easier terrain.

"Anyhow, that is all history, isn't it?"

"History never go away. Anyhow, what I want to say is that Shad was not very welcome when he come first. Perhaps if something bad happen at that time, you could look for one Yoruba boy who kill Shad because he *jealous* him."

"But not now?"

"Never now! Shad is our brother, and Jude is our brother. No Yoruba man lift his hand against him. Our tears are flowing for him everytime."

Molly also interviewed the orphan *pickin*. The child arrived, smiling up at her, his sparkling teeth and great luminous eyes lighting up his whole face. He sat shyly on a hard-back chair across the table from her, ankles crossed, hands joined on his bare knees. He could not be more than ten years of age, she thought.

"Good morning, Pita."

"Good night, Miss Policeman."

"What age are you?"

"Please?"

"What age are you, how old?"

"My old? I am fourteen and fifteen."

"What! You are too small."

"Miss, I try small!"

Molly discovered afterward that the child was at least fourteen. He had arrived a year previously to the North Wall in a Panamanian-registered merchant ship purportedly carrying plastic flanges for refrigeration units from Marseilles to Dublin. One of three survivors from a human cargo of nine found holed up in one of the plastic part containers, his only known family, an elder brother and a younger sister, lay dead to either side of him. The group was known to have come from the Delta region of Nigeria and Pita was Ijaw by tribe. Their journey, which had started in Port Harcourt and probably lasted upward of eight months, was a confused nightmare of sea voyages, exhausting treks through bush and jungle, and a long and terrifying burial alive in the dark, roasting, and suffocating container from which he had emerged an emaciated skeleton, starving, parched, and almost out of his child's mind. The children had been told that they were going to America to rejoin their father. There was no father. They were, in fact, almost certainly destined for a life of slavery or prostitution.

Molly, unaware of all this, had asked the child where his parents were.

"My father in America."

"And your mother?"

"Please?"

"Where is your mother?"

He remained perfectly motionless on his chair, looking straight into her face with solemn unblinking eyes, his expression grave as a judge. One great round tear, just one, welled from each eye and rolled down his cheeks in perfect symetry. He made no sound, neither speech nor cry.

That evening Molly told Jan-Hein about it:

"It was just how those two tears came—so simultaneously and so immediately: it was as if they are in there always and will always be there—and then his utter silence, as if nothing that could be said, not even crying, could express what he felt. The poor little mite!"

"Jesus Christ," exclaimed Jan-Hein, who was learning these Irish Catholic vocatives—as much prayer as profanity, "what a horrible story! I hope there is a special place in hell for people who do things like that to children."

"I thought you didn't believe in hell."

"For this, I make an exception."

A courageous and enlightened official had decided that, better than institutionalizing the child, they should leave him in the care of the African wider family. The tactic had worked perfectly. Pita had more mothers, fathers, and siblings than any child in Europe. They fed him, clothed him, taught him, and above all, loved him back to life. The O'Connell Schools had shown great flexibility about his gradual induction into the world of educa-tion. He was being individually tutored a few times a week by a cheerful young lady teacher who had got his wavelength. He was bright, and it was hoped that he would be able to start into first year secondary on a regular basis in the following September.

Meanwhile Pita roamed around the north inner city, a sort of Gavroche. People, black and white, knew his story and smiled to see him alive and well. Indeed he was probably the most recog-nized child and something of a mascot in the triangle between the Rotunda, the Four Courts, and O'Connell Bridge, where, ex-cept among black folk, the making of babies is a forgotten art.

Like most black children, Pita was observant. He had noticed Shad leaving the restaurant that Tuesday evening and knew it was unusual. Sometimes Shad might run out in his apron to buy a bottle of this or a tin of that. This time his clothes were "too de-cent" and he was walking right away from the restaurant. Shad was Pita's hero and his role model. When he grew up, he had al-ready decided, he would work in Shad's restaurant and marry Margot—that is, if Shad didn't mind.

That evening he had followed Shad. Perhaps he was going to visit Esther? But no, instead of going up toward Dorset Street and St. Savior's, he had turned down toward the river. When he got there he crossed the Ha'penny Bridge. Pita hesitated: South of the river was uncharted territory. He followed.

"Why did you follow him, Pita?"

"I no follow him, I come after. Is like game, like hunter; you see what you hunt, he no see you."

"Did you follow Shad over the bridge?"

"I no follow him, I come after. He go front small, into street on other side. There he meet one white man."

"Wait a moment. He goes on a bit—is that what you are saying?—and he meets a white man?"

"*E-heh!* Too big white man, ten feet," he added proudly, aware of Europeans' love for weights and measurements. "He have black head hair like vulture thieving meat in market."

"What age . . . what old?"

"Fourteen and fifteen."

"No, Pita, not you: the man, what old is the man?"

"He is too old. Five hundred, like Moses, like your fat police-man."

"Inspector Quilligan?" Molly asked, loving it. Wait till Jim hears this!

"*E-heh*, that one! He is too like the same for that one."

Molly was beginning to get the syntax and the vocabulary: the single, all-purpose tense, the almost biblical numbers system, the subtly different meaning of words. "To follow" does not mean to follow in our sense: it means to accompany. The adverb "too" doesn't mean excessively: it means "very." So, for instance, to tell someone that he is "too funny" is a compliment, not a put-down. If somebody trips and falls, you say "sorry," not by way of apology, as if you had toppled him yourself, but as a polite expression of sympathy. Molly found talking to Africans like reading poetry, not that their speech is particularly melodious, but because familiar words and phrases sound somehow fresh and meaningful, full of new color and nuance. It is like reading overfamiliar sacred texts in a foreign language: they come to life again.

Piecing together what Pita told her during a long and sometimes puzzling conversation, Molly was able to say that Shad, the night before he died, left his restaurant at about six o'clock, walked down to the river, crossed over into Temple Bar where he met a large-size, middle-aged man in the street, who had black, slicked-back hair and wore a dark suit. They seemed to know each other, but did not shake hands. They were neither over-friendly nor hostile. They walked together in silence to what was probably a multistory parking lot and went in. At that point the boy returned to his own side of the river.

Job number one, said Quilligan when he heard the report, find the good-looking fellow like me—except that he has black hair!

Jim Quilligan, on his watch, had been working his way through the regular customers of the restaurant, and also those of the adjoining hairdresser's and snooker hall. Nobody had any ideas about who might have killed Shad, or why. He was struck by the fact that there was no tendency among them to demonize white folk, even those who they knew disliked or despised them. Totally puzzled as they were, both by the fact and by the nature of the murder, they did not seem inclined to go hunting scapegoats. Quilligan eventually found himself almost inciting them to say that Shad had been killed by racists. Nobody rose to it. Instead, there was much resigned dropping of one upturned hand into the other, the African equivalent of shoulder-shrugging sad bewilderment.

All changed with the arrival of Fat Isaac, who made his entrance—rather than merely coming in—fully attired in traditional costume: stiff damask toga, the red bonnet and neckbeads of a chief, a ruler's white hair switch in his hand. Having enthroned himself as best he could on Pita's modest chair, he indicated by a gracious wave of his feathers that Quilligan had permission to speak.

"Mr. Isaac, can you—"

"*Chief* Isaac, Inspector, if you would."

He spoke with just the right mix of regret and gracious forgiveness for the inspector's lack of *savoir vivre*. "Chief" Isaac was an educated man who prided himself on his knowledge of English and of protocol—especially in matters touching the respect due to his own person.

"Well, Chief, a man of your importance and influence must be able to cast some light on this sad affair."

This was not Quilligan's natural way of speaking, but he had learned how to do it, and he also knew that it worked with people too vain to see through it. Chief Isaac did not disappoint him.

"You are a discriminating man, Inspector. And you are right. All these boys are too provincial to understand what is happening. And as for you people, you Irish police: this is an African affair. You have no chance at all of solving this mystery, unless I do it for you."

"Please do."

Chief Isaac's eyes narrowed. He realized that the inspector's invitation was a challenge. He wondered uncomfortably whether the policeman might not also be making fun of him.

"Inspector, Shad's foot was cut off. He was left to die. The person who did this probably intended his death, but only in the sense that he did not want him to live and tell his story. The cutting off of the foot was the main purpose of the exercise. Are you with me?"

Quilligan was impressed.

"I am with you."

"So what does that mean? In terms of modern European culture, it means nothing. I say in terms of *modern* European culture. Don't let's forget, all the same, that it is not two hundred years since the British were hanging children aged eight and the French were lopping off people's hands."

"Really?" Quilligan said, showing polite surprise that he did not feel.

"In terms of Nigerian society, this amputation could mean a number of things. It could be a legal punishment under Sharia law; that is the Koranic law of Islam."

"I've heard of it. Do they really cut off people's hands and feet?"

"Not often, but it happens—throughout the Arab world, in some Asian and African countries, as well. In Nigeria, this would be in some of the northern states, in Zamfara especially. It is usually the right hand that is cut off, as a punishment for thieves. I certainly know of a case in Zamfara where a cow thief had his hand cut off, and another one in Sokoto where a man who stole a goat got the same punishment. It is harsh but it is effective as a deterrent—more effective, believe me, than your Catholic nonsense: 'Three Hail Marys, and don't do it again'!"

"And what about cutting off somebody's leg or foot?"

"There is what they call cross-amputation. Right hand, left foot, both together." He made a swift, diagonal slicing gesture through the air. "There was a case in Sudan in 2003 where a sixteen-year-old boy, Mohammed Hassan Hamdan, was condemned to cross-amputation for armed robbery. I don't know if the sentence was carried out. These Amnesty International people—you know the ones who are always interfering in everything—they were making a fuss about it. The rascal probably got off."

"Do you mean you are in favor of that sort of thing?"

"I am in favor of law and order, and of whatever it takes."

Quilligan was tempted to get stuck in on that discussion. He stayed on subject.

"But Shad's case was a *right* foot amputation, and no hand."

"Yes. That is only one of many reasons for saying that his death had nothing to do with Sharia law. There are even more compelling reasons for that conclusion. Firstly, these Koranic amputations are unheard of in southern Nigeria, where Shad came from—regrettably: they could do with a few choppings from time to time down there, as a warning to bandits. Secondly, there are certainly no amputations being practiced by Muslims here in Dublin, and, thirdly, nobody could possibly suspect Shad of stealing or indeed of any criminal activity. For a Christian and a Catholic, he was an unusually upright young man."

"So why are we talking about Sharia?"

"We must cover all the possibilities, Inspector. Did they not teach you that in police school?"

Quilligan smiled, less at the impertinence of the question than at the thought of how little he did of all that he had been taught to do in police school. His method had never been to cover all the possibilities: his way was to go with his intuition—which was why he had found the time he had wasted over recent weeks with brainless facists a crucifying irrelevance. Now, convinced that at last he might be onto something, he smiled and said nothing.

Chief Isaac, disappointed, fanned himself unnecessarily with his hairy switch, readjusted the outworks of his ceremonial robes, and continued.

"Shad and his brother are from the Onitsha region. Onitsha is a large, lively and, some would say, a chaotic city. Like any large city in the southern half of Nigeria, where they do *not* have the benefits of Sharia, Onitsha is subject to outbreaks of total lawlessness. For months on end, armed robbers roam the streets at will, terrorizing the people, and especially the traders in the big market, taxing them of nearly all their profits, leaving them just enough to stay in business, so that the robbers can come back again and again to eat more money. This affects the whole city. Onitsha is, in fact, one big market, starting at the Niger Bridge and rolling away miles and miles to the east. There they will sell you *anything*. I guarantee you, Inspector, if you ask for a Boeing 757, some Igbo boy will bring it out from under the counter. So there are plenty of rich pickings for the parasite criminals who feed off the traders."

"Well, what about the police? What are they doing about it?"

"Inspector, I was a policeman for ten years, before I got enough money to travel out and get myself an education. Do you know how I got that money to travel out?"

"How?"

"Don't ask, Inspector, don't ask. Just take my word for it. There are many good men and women in the Nigerian police force, but they are—how do you say it?—checkmated by the bad cops and the armed robbers. I am sad to tell you: in my country, if armed robbers are staying a long time in one place, it is because they have police protection. The police are eating money, too. In Nigeria, nobody cheats the system, because cheating *is* the system. So I got the money together and bought my education. Now I can afford the luxury of being honest."

Quilligan shook his big head.

"Bad scene, Chief, but what has this got to do with Shad?"

"Some years ago the governor of Anambra State got desperate about the lawlessness in Onitsha. He could do nothing about it through the normal channels. So he decided on a desperate remedy. He brought in the Bakassi Boys."

"Who are the Bakassi Boys?" the inspector asked obediently.

"They come from Aba in Abia state. That is another town, not too far away from Onitsha. The Bakassi Boys are a sort of cult or secret society. They have magic powers. They can smell armed robbers hidden in a crowd, they pick them out and torture them until they confess their crimes. Then they kill them—their own special way. They give them a choice, long cut or short cut."

"What's that?"

"It's a choice of two ways to die. You don't want to know."

"God's sake, man! This is not serious."

"No? The boys who get killed think it is very serious—if you can judge by their shrieks of agony. I saw one such execution. Believe me, my friend, it was *very* serious."

"But this business about being able to *smell* out the robbers . . . that is bullshit!"

"Please yourself, Inspector, but the men the Bakassi Boys pick out make full confessions of all that they had done, in the tiniest details, including robberies that nobody had accused them of."

"Well, of course! If a guy is being tortured he will admit anything."

"But they found the right robbers. Within a few months there were no more crimes. You could leave your car parked in the middle of the city, with the windows open and the doors unlocked. Nobody would put a finger near it."

"I hate your logic, man, it is dangerous! But, anyhow, what has this got to do with Shad?"

"Well, Onitsha is his place, and 'long cut' would include severing a leg—or two."

"Jesus! But not with an anesthetic?"

"No, of course not. But these boys are specialists in slow death, with plenty of crying. This is hard to do in the middle of Dublin. Suppose they took Shad by surprise, cut off his leg, under anesthetic—to keep him quiet, then left him up in the mountains to wake up and do his crying until he died."

"Are you suggesting that these Bonkers Boys—or whatever you called them—actually followed Shad here to Dublin to cut off his leg?"

"Inspector, a Nigerian will follow you to hell if necessary. You will not escape the Bakassi Boys."

"But you are the one who says that these Bakassi Boys are always right, and, on the other hand, you agreed with me that Shad is clean, or was clean."

"Clean? Well, that is what I think. But I also think that the Bakassi Boys do not make mistakes."

"So?"

"So, I do not think that the Bakassi Boys killed Shad."

"Here we go again! Why have we been talking about this, if . . ."

"I am surprised at you, Inspector, you have just spent hours and days, possibly weeks, talking to pathetic idiots who you must know had nothing to do with this thing, but you get impatient when I start to point you toward some real possibilities."

"Well, all right, but I haven't heard anything yet even remotely likely."

"Was Shad's murder even remotely likely, Inspector?"

"No, it wasn't. So how many more remotely likely explanations have you got?"

"Well, there is also the OPC," Isaac offered.

"I suppose this is where I say: 'Oh, and who are the OPC?'"

"Never mind, Inspector. I don't think we need bother about the OPC. They are the same sort of group as the Bakassi, but they are confined to the southwest of Nigeria. Shad is southeast."

"Thanks be to God for small mercies! Chief Isaac, like a decent man, will you answer me one straight question: Do you think you know who killed Shad Okafor, and, if you do think you know—who the hell is it?"

Chief Isaac rose to his feet, redeploying his robes about his person for best dramatic effect. Not looking at Quilligan, because great chiefs do not speak directly to lesser mortals, he addressed himself in confidential tones to some imaginary grand vizier at his side, who, presumably, was charged with promulgating his wisdom to the world's great unwashed. The wisdom on this occasion consisted of one word spoken very softly.

"Ogboni."

"What?"

"Ogboni," he repeated, in an even lower register.

"Ogboni, ogboni!" Quilligan exclaimed loudly, at the end of his patience, "What or who the hell is 'ogboni'?"

He realized afterward that he had been almost shouting. Instantly the chief's demeanor changed. From complacently majestic, he was suddenly furtive and afraid. The change was dramatic.

"Inspector, keep your voice down, please!" he hissed, darting nervous glances at the door.

Before he had finished speaking, the door opened. It was Tunde, the Yoruba owner of the snooker hall. There was no doubt that he had heard Quilligan's raucous question, and equally, no mistaking the hostility of the stare he fixed upon Fat Isaac. His words, sullen, even menacing, were addressed to Quilligan, but unambiguously meant for Chief Isaac, as well.

"Inspector, I'll answer your question. Ogboni is a friendly society of Nigerian people in all walks of life. It was originally associated with the religious beliefs of my own Yoruba tribe, but it is open to all people now. Ogboni had nothing, I repeat, *nothing* to do with Shad's death."

The last words were pronounced slowly and with emphasis. He went on: "Stop showing off, Fat Isaac, and telling your spiteful lies, or you will soon find out what Ogboni can do."

Chief Isaac, if he was a chief, can seldom have looked less chieftainly. Sprawled back shapelessly on his wooden chair, his fat belly wobbling between stumpy thighs, all his finery and feathers suddenly drooping, he was clearly terrified. His smooth English had deserted him.

"Ah no, Tunde, you hear bad. Ogboni very harmless people, very good, very kind, very . . ."

Quilligan was intrigued. He chuckled provocatively.

"Well, well! Praising Ogboni sounds like hard work, Chief Isaac. You're all out of nice words already!"

He turned to the snooker hall keeper.

"Do you mind? We are nearly finished."

The Yoruba went out. Quilligan got no further with Chief Isaac, whose one concern now was to put as much distance as he could between himself and Ogboni anger.

"No, Inspector, I was joking when I said I could solve this case for you—surely you understood that! About Ogboni, I just mentioned them in the same way as OPC or the Bakassi Boys, or even Sharia. I was just saying that this is like an African thing, not a white man thing. I was trying to sketch in a whole cultural background for you."

"Yes, thank you. That is interesting and I have taken it on board. But I am not a fool. I *know* what you said and you *did* say that you could solve the mystery for me. When I asked you to get finished with all those lists of people who *did not* kill Shad, and to tell me who *did* kill him, you stood up there, solemn as a prosecuting counsel, and you said: 'Ogboni.' Now I want to know why you said that and what you meant."

It ended badly, with Quilligan breaking all the rules. He threatened Fat Isaac with years in jail for being an accessory to a murder, for concealing evidence, for obstructing the police, for misprison of felony—though he couldn't quite remember what that one was about, but it sounded good. He also, inconsistently with his stated esteem for due process, menaced him with imminent transportation back across the seas to "wherever the hell" he came from.

None of this cut ice with Isaac. Such dire punishments were mere party games compared with what the Yorubas might do to him for even mentioning Ogboni.

Near to midnight the same day, Molly Power and her ever-loving Jan-Hein turned away from their home computer, boggle-eyed and weary. They were confident that they had discovered a reason why Fat Isaac had named Ogboni as Shad's killers and a reason—the *same* reason—why he was scared out of his skin that the same Ogboni would come to hear of his rashness.

Back in his Store Street office, Jim Quilligan gave Molly a wickedly satirical account of his discussion with Fat Isaac. Molly regaled Jan-Hein with it when she got home and they talked about it all through dinner, flying innumerable wild theories and shooting them down again.

"Hey!" Jan-Hein said on an impulse, as they stood up from the table. "Let's ask Old Mother Google!"

"What would you search under?"

"I'll just type in 'Ogboni.' What else?"

He went over to their PC and typed in the word.

"You won't get anything there."

"Probably not, but anyhow, let's . . . holy God, Molly, there are pages of stuff!"

There were indeed pages, and what a story they told Ogboni: Yoruba Secret Society, for the rich and the powerful, the movers and shakers, the makers and breakers of Nigerian society. Their history and cults, their magical and mystical practices and beliefs, their methods and punishments. Ogboni made presidents and princes, emirs and *obas*, governors and generals, perhaps even bishops and cardinals. Ogboni made them all, and broke them all. One day, a messenger would arrive to each of these potentates to say that his time had come. Then there was no choice, no argument, and no escape. He took poison and died.

Molly and Jan-Hein skimmed through as much as they could, printing out pages of it to be studied later. Toward the end of the evening, one hideous sequence leaped off the screen at them, one they would have no trouble remembering even without a printed reminder.

An Ogboni Punishment: The victim is chained to a bed in a cell. His foot is passed through a hole in the wall into an adjoining cell where executioners set to work to scrape all the skin, flesh, muscle, ligaments, veins, grissle, nerves, and whatever else there is, off that foot, until, clean as the proverbial whistle, nothing remains except the bare white bone.

"Sacred heart of Jesus," Molly exclaimed, "how could any human being do that to another person?"

"I don't know, sweetheart, but if that is what Fat Isaac thinks these Ogboni guys did to your Shad—I mean an adapted version of that punishment—it is no wonder he is scared out of his tree that they might come after him for more of the same."

Molly thought about it.

"Perhaps not all the Yoruba were as happy as Tunde to see Shad set up a thriving Igbo business in Yoruba territory. Perhaps the Ogboni were punishing him for this offense. Jim will be disgusted—and fascinated—to hear all this."

CHAPTER SIX

"Y<small>OU MUST BE</small> J<small>UDE</small>," <small>SHE SAID, SURPRISED.</small>

"Yes, I am Jude. I had to come to see you."

"Come in, Jude, you are welcome."

It had not been difficult at all. He had followed Margot's instructions: Take the Forty-six bus from City Centre, pay as you get in, sit upstairs, and enjoy the view. When you see Foxrock Church at the bottom of the hill, come down and get out at the next stop, cross the road—be careful: it is very busy—and go up Westminster Road. You are there.

"You are so like Shad. Poor Shad, he was such a lovely boy: so manly, so mannerly. That sounds stupid, doesn't it? 'Manly and mannerly': it is so hit-and-miss, so incomplete as to be almost insulting. Just, somehow, it sparks off Shad's memory for me. Does it say anything to you?"

"I hear it."

"But you don't agree, you think it is not enough."

"No, I hear it. I *hear* it. That means I hear it very well. I hear it inside my heart."

"I am glad."

"I come, first time, to say thank, thank, thank you for what you and your husband did for Shad's funeral. May God bless you for that one. I could never have done it without you."

"It was a pleasure for us, the only small thing we could do in so great a tragedy."

"Please, can you show me pictures of Shad?"

She smiled at him tenderly.

"But, of course. Why didn't I think of that? You probably have no picture of him."

"One photograph, too terrible!"

"I probably have several sketches of his body parts. Forgive me; that sounds awful in the circumstances. What I mean is that I used him a lot to practice anatomy. So, I have forearms, shoulder muscles, rib cage. He had very clean lines . . . I am sorry, we should not be talking this way, as if he had been totally carved up."

"Have you no picture of all of him . . . altogether?"

"Come along, let's go down to the studio and let's see what I have." She stood up and led the way, down a stairs into the base-ment, along a corridor, out into a secluded and surprisingly spa-cious back garden, then along a crazy pavement to an open-plan dacha-style studio at the farthest end from the house. He watched her as she went. She was, he thought, a beautiful woman. Obvi-ously careful about her appearance, she looked thirty-something, though he knew she was probably in her late fifties.

Jude reflected that he was seeing Mrs. Finnerty exactly like she, as an artist, had seen Shad—good body parts. She had good body parts: there was no denying that, but he did not feel at-tracted to her emotionally or sexually. He felt sure that, whatever the relationship between Shad and this woman, he had not ro-manced her . . . unless . . . no! He was certain: Shad would not sell his body for money, not *that* way—although he had sold it for painting. That cannot have been easy, for a man to take off his clothes for a woman, for a black man to take off his clothes for a white woman—and remain completely passive. He wondered how Shad had done it. Jude could not imagine himself taking off his clothes, *any* clothes, for this white woman.

Lost in these thoughts, Jude barely registered that they had entered the studio. He was aware of a spacious room full of light, two or three easels, drawings and paintings pinned to hardboard screens, several greatly enlarged black-and-white photographs, as well. There were tables and trolleys with jars and sticks, tubes, which he presumed must be paints, brushes of all sizes, scalpels, sandpaper, and art paper of various textures and dimensions: a lot of stuff, but organized and tidy in a loose kind of way. Down at the end of the studio was an area for what looked like pottery work or sculpture of some kind.

She was searching through art portfolios and in drawers. He sat down mechanically on a camp chair. When she came over behind him and spoke suddenly, he jumped, startled and embarrassed: he had just reached the stage of refusing, in his thoughts, to take his clothes off.

"A penny for them!"

"A penny for what?" he asked in something like terror.

"For your thoughts."

The blood rushed to his face. Black people *do* blush and get sunburned. White people don't notice it. He was sure that she *did* notice and that she knew what he had been thinking. Before he could check himself he had blurted out:

"I was wondering why Shad . . . why he was doing this thing . . ."

She drew up a stool and sat down. Smiling, she took his hands and held them on his knee. He found that disconcerting.

"I understand. Well, Jude, just in case you are wondering—and I know that you are—the relationship between Shad and myself was very *proper*. I think that is the word. His sensibilities on these things, if you understand what I mean, were very much the same as your own. I never asked Shad to be . . . fully naked."

She continued more lightly:

"So I never did get those pelvic muscles quite right! I have a David and Goliath out there somewhere—in America, I think—and they both look like they have double hernias!"

Jude had no idea what she was talking about.

"How did it begin?"

"Very simply. My husband employs one or two Nigerian boys in his funeral business, driving hearses, dressing up bodies nicely, whatever. He sent one of these boys here one day to collect something he had forgotten. The lad, quite against the rules, I should add, brought his friend, Shad, for the ride: Shad had never been farther south than the Grand Canal."

"I hadn't been that far my very self until today."

"Anyhow, the minute I saw Shad, I knew he was perfect. I said to myself, My God, this is my Wilson! He *must* model for me; I'll pay gold bars!"

"And did you?" he asked seriously.

"Did I what?"

"Did you pay gold bars?"

She laughed.

"'Pay gold bars' is just an expression, but I did pay him well."

"Who is this Wilson?"

"Wilson was a young black American, from Boston, I think. He came to England as a sailor in about 1810. A doctor, who treated him for some minor injury, noted that he was perfect from an artist's point of view. That doctor knew what he was talking about. His name was Anthony Carlisle and he was professor of anatomy at the Royal Academy. So, through him, every painter and sculptor in England got to hear about Wilson. They didn't put him in pictures very much. At the time, that would have been . . . unusual."

"Because he was black?"

"Well, yes, to be honest; it wasn't the fashion. There were strange theories going around about, umm . . . let's say the different racial types. But they used him all the time to practice drawing human anatomy. He earned a lot of money."

"Then, when they have learn very well, they paint white what they have learn black, and put that one in the pictures?"

"Well, I'm afraid, yes; that's about it. His color is not really emphasized in the surviving drawings—and we have almost no picture of his face."

"So that is why you have no picture of Shad, except his ribs and his elbow, and such like, because he was a nigger with fat lips and wide nose?"

He felt immediately that he was mean to say that. Shad would never have said it. People are entitled to be limited and stupid; and she was trying. . . .

"No, Jude, no! I did not think about Shad like that. I am not prejudiced. Well, I hope I am not. I certainly have sketches somewhere of Shad's head and face, because I did use him, once or twice, in finished paintings. Let me find them. Then, I promise you, I will do a beautiful portrait of Shad for you. It will be a labor of love."

"Will you do one for my mother?"

She paused, more impressed than annoyed with his directness. He obviously had no idea what she usually charged for a portrait, not to mention two!

"Yes, Jude, I will."

"Show me a picture of Wilson . . . please."

She stood up and went over to some shelves where there was an extensive library of expensive-looking art books. Out of a set of four or five large volumes in white dust jackets, she selected one and brought it back. The title read *The Image of the Black in Western Art.* It was published, he saw, by Harvard University in the United States.

"Look at this, Jude, it is a marvelous collection. It gives a complete record of pictures, sculptures, pottery, every sort of image of black people made in the Western world, from the time of the pharoahs in Egypt, right up to the First World War. Actually, volume three has never been published, but I have all the rest. I picked them up, one at a time, on websites specializing in rare and out-of-print books."

Jude took the volume on his knees while Mrs. Finnerty went off to make tea. There were two or three pictures of Wilson, all nudes. In one he was sitting on the ground with his back to the viewer. He was resting on his extended left arm and drawing in his ankles with the other arm, his knees up to his chest. Jude could see how this pose showed up the long curve of the man's backbone from his neck to the base of his spine. Apart from that he could see no point in it at all. The other picture showed a muscular man wrestling with a big cow—or what the book called a "buffalo." This amazed him. Imagine wrestling with a cow—and with no clothes on! It did not make sense. He could see nothing remarkable about Wilson. If he was indeed a black man, you would need to be told this: it was not obvious.

Perhaps the text would enlighten him, he thought. Jude could read quite well but he could make nothing of what was written in this book.

> Even when the arm was bent, the olecranon instead of making disagreeable angles, as in other meagre forms . . . was buried . . . beautifully within the line—This seemed to be the principle; that everything was packed in.

What could that possibly mean? He understood every single word—except "olecranon"—but the whole thing together said nothing. And what could anybody make of what came on the next page?

> Haydon measured the proportions of Wilson's body— "He was 7 heads & ¾; his half below his pubis—the third head ends at his navel . . ."

He could not understand even the punctuation, which seemed as weird as the text. What kind of a monster was this, with seven and three-quarter heads, one of them growing out of his navel! It was as incomprehensible as parts of the Book of Revelation in the Bible, which he had read earnestly but could never understand.

Tiring of Wilson, Jude began to leaf through the pictures in the rest of the book. As he did so, horror invaded his soul. Where this woman saw wonderful examples of European and American art, Jude saw one picture after another of black slaves, in rags or stark naked, being hunted with dogs, chained, sold, whipped, branded, abused in every way by cruel-faced white men, and even by other black men, dissolute, hideous ones, who had sold their souls to their brutal masters.

There were also pictures of black people in beautiful clothes, mostly Muslim types, rulers, obviously wealthy and important people, but they were not enough to undo the impact of those terrible images of his people's degradation. These had struck him like a blow in the face.

Jude had grown up in a society where there were few books and fewer pictures. Images had a very powerful impact on his imagination and feelings. The first time he had seen a pornographic film in Lagos, he had been utterly shocked; and the damage could not be undone The unimaginable had become imaginable, and those images of lust were burned into his soul forever. He felt that he had lost his innocence and that these phantoms would seduce and torment him until the day he died.

Now tears of shame and distress pricked at his eyes for what these images were revealing to him: the humiliation of his race. He had known about the slave trade, of course—they had learned it in school—but he had no idea of the bestial reality as he saw it pictured here.

She saw his dismay when she came back and understood her mistake. She did not force him to drink tea. He left almost immediately.

That night Jude had horrible dreams. The undertaker's wife was tearing his clothes off and pulling him onto her, to romance her—no, not her—but her body parts, one by one, a hand, between her toes, an armpit, her horrible lipsticked mouth opening like a hole into hell. She was pulling him onto her and screaming: "Do my olecranon, do my olecranon!" He was horrified and violently aroused.

He woke before dawn, crying out, his body drenched with his own sweat and semen.

Superintendent Denis Lennon was the head of the Murder Squad and a good friend of both Jim Quilligan and Molly Power. Molly had worked with him regularly for six or seven years, when he still handled individual cases himself. Now in his sixties, and not in wonderful health, he confined himself mostly to a supervisory and organizational role. He was good at human relations, handled the press well, and protected his team against predators, meaning smart-ass lawyers, politicians, and rival camps within the law-enforcement agencies.

Lennon was exasperated by the financial cutback policy that sent Molly Power out cruising around on general squad car patrols whenever the murderers were slacking on the job. On the other hand, he realized that the tide that goes out always comes in. Lennon had to acknowledge that the same fiscal policies that occasionally deprived him of Molly, even more often brought him the services of Inspector Jim Quilligan.

Jim, who was descended from a distinguished line of itinerant art dealers, was nominally the head of his own art-crime section in the Gardaí. Formed to the task genetically and by osmosis, he was also self-taught and was knowledgeable, both about art and about who to ask and where to look when things got stolen, faked, or sold on. There was a European, even an international dimension to the job, because that is how the market is. Nevertheless Ireland did not have enough accessible art to generate enough crime to keep a full-time Quilligan credible. His job was a nice idea, but he had no staff and little funding, and was often "loaned out" to other sections. He had worked on at least one important murder case with Lennon and was happy to be back on his team at any time.

The three were having a conference about Shad's case. Jim

and Molly had been telling Denis all about the Bakassi Boys, the law of Sharia, and especially the leg-scratching activities of the Ogboni. Lennon beamed good-naturedly.

"Seems to me we could do with all three of them in this country. But seriously, where are we at?"

"Well, Molly has sure done her homework on the Ogboni crowd. It may all sound a tall story to our way of thinking, but the murder itself, or the attack, if you prefer, is so off-the-wall, the explanation has got to be something equally weird."

"But the anesthetic; that is the weirdest thing of all. All your possible explanations, whether Irish explanations, like racism, or African explanations, like Bakassi and Ogboni—they all aim at pain or punishment. It is the anesthetic which brings them all tumbling down."

Molly answered:

"Yes, that is how we reasoned at the beginning. We think now that the anesthetic was probably not a suppression of pain and punishment, but a postponement."

"Postponement, how do you mean?"

"This may even be some indication of where the assault took place."

"You've lost me seriously!"

"What Molly means, Denis, is that whoever took off that foot could not afford to have a lot of screaming and shouting going on—because of the neighbors, let's say! Also he probably had nobody or not enough people to hold the victim down while he did his chopping, sawing, or whatever the hell they do. So he knocks the guy out, takes off his foot, then drives him up the Dublin Mountains and leaves him in a deserted place—as he thought—to wake up and have his pain and punishment until he dies in agony of . . . Christ, you know what I mean. The shit, whoever he was!"

Lennon tugged at his earlobe and made soft kissing sounds to help his thinking.

"It does look like an African thing, doesn't it? The strangeness of the punishment: that is from another culture altogether. Then, the screaming bit, and not disturbing the neighbors. Most of these Africans still live in semighetto conditions, a lot of people piled into a small space. I don't suppose you could do a wide-awake amputation in there without exciting some small degree of curiosity."

Molly added another argument.

"Whoever dumped the victim didn't know the Dublin Mountains very well. The Murtaghs' house is not all that visible, and indeed, Jim and I had trouble finding it; but nobody accustomed to the general topography would think of that place as deserted. There are houses within a half a mile or less."

"That doesn't prove it was an African who dumped the body."

"No, but it does seem to rule out anyone who knows the mountain or who is used to that kind of terrain. I am not a Dub myself, but I am sure I could have found a better place to off-load a body."

Lennon tugged his other ear and made more kissing noises.

"I'll tell you what I'll do. It is not much, but it may get you on a right track. I'll consult my wife's uncle. He was a Holy Ghost missionary in Nigeria for umpteen years, until the end of the Biafran War. Then they were all thrown in prison, and eventually put out."

"Why? Was he gunrunning?"

"I doubt it. It is a sad story, really. The Holy Ghost missionaries had evangelized the whole eastern region of Nigeria. Naturally, when the war came, they stayed with their people and, I suppose, took their side. What do you expect? The Igbo soldiers were kids they had baptized, altar boys who had served their Masses. They couldn't just stand by and see them die, not to mention the sufferings of the civilian population.

"It was a cruel war—on both sides—and the end was not magnanimous. Especially in the Igbo towns west of the Niger, there were pogroms. By then nobody was thinking right. The missionaries were lucky to get away with their lives but, practically to a man, they were expelled, never to return. Mike eventually came to see it as providential. It was time for the white missionaries to go, he says, and to let the local church take over. Anyhow, let me ask him."

"What will you ask him?"

"Well, about Ogboni and all that stuff. I know he has been out of the country for years but he has excellent contacts. He'll know who to ask. Besides, at the gut level, I bet he still knows more than half the egghead academics teaching African Studies in universities around the world."

Quilligan nodded.

"I could believe that. Give it a whirl, Denis."

"Yes," agreed Molly. "The missionaries have a phrase: 'You can take the man out of Africa, you cannot take Africa out of the man.' Your Uncle Mike will probably say something useful!"

Jude's violent dreams of the night hung over him all day like a dark cloud. Jude had never sexed a girl. He accepted the strict moral code of his upbringing, traditional African and Christian. He did not know how long this would last, especially in his present vulnerable condition. He knew that chastity had not been completely possible for Shad, although he, too, did try. What he was sure of was that he wanted any sexual relationship he might have with a girl in the future to be face to face, body to body, whole person to whole person. What he had done, or been forced to do, in his dream—jerking off on somebody else's body parts—

seemed to him degrading and depraved. In the context of Shad's death by amputation, it upset him deeply.

And the anger? Where did the violent rage he had felt in his dream come from? What did it mean? He had quite liked Mrs. Finnerty when he met her, though he had not found her sexually attractive. There was nothing unusual about that. She was, after all, more than twice his age. There was also all that stuff about Shad taking off his clothes, his passivity before a woman in the role of artist's model. Add to that again Mrs. Finnerty's concentration on body parts—the way she had carved up Shad with her artist's scalpel—and the whole Wilson theme: how he, too, had been carved up, his face and his blackness, his true identity as a person, ignored and denied. And, finally, those awful pictures of slavery, the sheer indignity of it, the degradation. Obscurely, Jude knew that it was not so much the dream that was upsetting him as the intertwining of all these things with Shad's death. He had thought that he was coping well with Shad's murder but, scratch the surface, and down in his secret mind, in the depths of his heart, was this seething, writhing nest of poison vipers.

He would have liked to talk to Margot about it, but how could he? He would die of shame and embarrassment to use the words he would have to use. Besides, he did not even know half the words he would need, in English or in any language. The only persons he could ever have spoken to about such things—because they would understand without words—were his mother, who was so far away, and Shad, who was . . . He covered his face with his hands.

A thought came to him much later when he was going to bed, utterly exhausted, after one of the most difficult days of his entire life. Perhaps all this means something, perhaps it is going somewhere. He would just have to hang in there somehow and hope. Perhaps this mess is what grieving is really about: not just all those sad thoughts going through his head, but this *wound*, this *weakness* deep in his spirit and pervading everything, thoughts, emotions, even his virgin sexuality. If this was, somehow, what he was going through for love of Shad, and for love of love, he accepted it; he would not disown it or be ashamed of it. He fell asleep almost immediately and slept soundly.

Pita, the orphan *pickin*, had moved his headquarters to deep behind enemy lines, which means south of the river. He had heard the Dubs themselves talking about "Northsiders" and "Southsiders" and the animosity between the two. Apparently, these were two warring tribes who lived on opposite sides of the river Liffey. He had heard their secret incantations, some of which he could repeat though he did not understand them, because they were secret. Like for instance:

Q. *What is a Northsider in a suit?*
A. *The accused.*

Or:

Q. *What is a Northsider in a wedding dress?*
A. *Pregnant.*

There must have been some sort of truce in operation since before Pita's arrival in Dublin, as he had not seen much fighting— except on Friday and Saturday nights when they would all congregate in a sacred space called Temple Bar, to drink, to fight, and to vomit. Other people were allowed to join in, which Pita thought was peculiar. When they were all finished drinking, fighting, and vomiting, the ambulances came and carted them off to the hospitals where they lay on trolleys for eleven hours. Nature heals, of course. In Dublin at weekends, She did not have much competition.

The river, Pita thought, was quite inadequate to keep warring factions apart. Dublin really needed a serious river, like the Niger, or else a maze of waterways, like in the delta where he came from, and where surprise was the major factor in warfare. Pita knew hundreds of secret streams and hidden inlets. He could negotiate these in the pitch dark in a canoe that he could swivel and turn on a five-*kobo* piece. He was also an excellent marksman with bow and arrow, having once killed a crocodile outright with one brilliant shot. That was just as well, because his bolt once shot, it would have been the crocodile's turn next.

He had the makings of a warrior, if only he could grow up a little. He was too small. It didn't matter for the moment. He did not want to be a warrior here in Dublin where warriors had no dignity. Imagine fighting with bottles and bricks, or assassins' knives, instead of with noble weapons like swords and spears. Besides, he could not understand all this vomiting. Perhaps it was a primitive form of divination. It would never occur to his own people to read somebody's destiny out of their vomit.

He knew he was taking a risk moving south of the river. Through the accident of his arrival by sea to the North Wall, he was a Northsider. If hostilities broke out again suddenly and he was not quick enough back across the Ha'penny Bridge, he would be spoils of war. What would they do to him? They might use him for sacrifice, or even eat him. He did not think that they would eat him. He had too little meat. God is marvelous! See how he protects his children by making them not have too much meat!

On the other hand, they might bury his head with a *taoiseach* or with one of their big chiefs. Big chiefs need many slaves in the other world. In his own country, it was said that an important *oba* would be buried with a hundred heads or more. As soon as the ruler died, the warriors had to collect these heads as quickly and in whatever way they could. They took criminals, prisoners of war, strangers, children on their way home from school or who had gone to the stream to fetch water. They seized drivers whose cars broke down or who had stopped a moment to urinate on the side of the road. The police looked the other way. The federal authorities knew that it did not pay to interfere with local traditions.

Perhaps these were old wives' tales. The burial was done secretly by the traditional priests and high palace officials, so no ordinary person could ever say that they had seen all these heads go down. The fact was nevertheless that whenever a big chief died, the mothers ran to collect their children from the school and would not let them out of the compound again until that chief was safely buried. Some chiefs took their wives with them when they died. Others, curiously, did not.

So why would Pita take this enormous risk? For one simple reason: for love of Shad. He would roam those streets, early and late, until he saw the man again who had taken Shad away the night when they killed him.

Superintendant Denis Lennon called Jim Quilligan on Sunday evening. This was unusual. Denis was a Lord's Day observance man. He went to Mass in the late morning, and spent the rest of the day with his wife, at home or with their married children and grandchildren. He did nothing about crime on Sunday, unless he had to, his stated rationale being that the bad guys would still be there on Monday morning. But Jim Quilligan was a friend, and he had news for him. A little phone call would do no harm.

"Two things, Jim, conveniently interconnected. I went up to see Uncle Mike in Kimmage Manor on Friday. He is retired up there. Eighty-four, he says he is."

"Good man; how is he?"

"Dangerously well."

"Marvelous! And what did he say?"

"Perhaps we can meet tomorrrow, and I'll give you the detailed version. Here is the summary. Ogboni is a serious and powerful force. Many of the movers and shakers in business and politics belong, and these people do not talk about it, do not dare to talk about it. The result of that is twofold. First, there are plenty of mysteries—some of them possibly sinister. On the other hand, there are probably twice as many cock-and-bull stories going around about them, because no outsider really knows what he is talking about."

"Inconvenient, but it makes sense."

"Mike says that, whatever about some local dude here in Dublin using the name 'Ogboni' for his own personal vanity and vendettas, it is most unlikely that the big boys in Ibadan, or wherever they are, would have the remotest interest in some poor devil with a fish and chip shop here in Dublin."

"Not fish and chips, Denis. Beware! I speak from firsthand experience."

"Thanks. Don't tell me. Anyhow, Father Mike said he would make a few inquiries and ring me back—which he did, last night."

"And?"

"And—wait for it—if you are really interested, you will have to go to Nigeria. You'll need yellow fever—I mean the shots, not the disease . . ."

"Hold on, Denis, have you taken leave of your senses?"

"I'm telling it like it is. I am telling you like I was told. Mike says that there is some guy—I have the name written down somewhere. Anyhow this guy is a university professor in a place called Ekpoma. It seems he knows everything about Ogboni."

"From the inside?"

"It also seems: you don't ask him that."

"But will he talk?"

"To you? No way! But if you are accompanied by an SMA priest called Dick Dorr, it's like open sesame: the guy talks. I know Dick. He has been out there for years. Lovely chap; he inspires confidence."

"God, I don't know, Denis. I wouldn't be sure enough of my ground to say that such a trip is justified. The Ogboni is just one possible line of inquiry."

"Do you have any others?"

"Well, just now, no, actually."

"I said I had a second thing to tell you."

"There is more?"

"There is. For once, cutbacks may do someone a favor. There is a United Nations conference coming up on child trafficking worldwide, you know, slavery, prostitution, all that stuff."

"Yes, I heard. Sheila Hegarty is going."

"Precisely. She is not. She is pregnant and over forty. Her obstetrician says 'no way!' He has impounded her. So they are looking for someone to go. Guess what: the jamboree is in Benin City, Nigeria. It seems an awful lot of the children, girls mostly, are coming from that region. Anyhow, the idea of two birds with one

stone—the child conference *and* a murder inquiry—will entrance the skinflints in Finance, especially as travel to and from
the Benin thing is being covered by the UN."

"Nigeria is a huge country."

"It is, but I've checked that out for you, too. Ekpoma, where
the professor with all the lore on Ogboni lives, is an hour from
Benin City, and Onitsha, where your boys come from, is less
than two hours. Mike says that the roads, which were terrible in
his time, are now fine."

"I'll think about it, Denis."

"Think quick: you are leaving tomorrow night."

"Jesus, Mary, and Joseph!"

"The UN will fix your visa. Bring your passport in to me tomorrow. I'll look after it, and your plane tickets, and I'll have
money for you. Sterling or dollars is best. Then go up to the Tropical Unit at the old College of Surgeons—down beyond the Gai-
ety Theatre—they will be waiting for you."

"For what?"

"Yellow fever, hepatitis A to Z, malaria pills, possibly meningi-
tis, typhoid, polio, and TB."

"Mother of God, I'll be like a pincushion."

"Cheer up, they'll probably let you off the cholera. It doesn't
work anyhow. They will also lecture you about your sex life and
about unboiled, unfiltered water. If you have any doubt about the
water, stick to beer."

"That's the first sensible suggestion you've made."

CHAPTER SEVEN

Fat Isaac had sought to create an impression. It was a matter of habit. What never seemed to become a habit, in spite of innumerable reminders, was the realization that he had failed once more and made himself ridiculous yet again. To the contrary, on this occasion, as on many others, he was fully sure that he *had* made an impression—but, unfortunately, of the wrong kind and in the wrong quarter. He had hoped to fascinate the white policeman with his detailed knowledge of tropical mysteries; instead, he had infuriated the Yoruba man with his virtual indictment of the Ogboni secret society. This was not a good thing to have done.

The Yoruba tribe ruled this neck of the jungle. To speak disrespectfully, not to mention accusingly, of Ogboni was dangerous and foolish. The foolish bit was not Chief Isaac's doing, of course: it was entirely the fault of that stupid detective with the great red face and the camel's head of hair. He had been shouting the name of Ogboni so loud that Tunde Akintole had heard it outside and come running in. He had summed up the situation at a glance: Fat Isaac was dishing the dirt on Ogboni. If the police believed him, or even half believed him, the result could be a major descent of the locusts on the Yoruba colony in Dublin.

Dozens, perhaps hundreds, would be found to have no proper papers to be in employment, to be living where they were, to be availing of social welfare, to be engaged in trading, driving cars, owning television sets, or even to be in Ireland at all. Others, or the same ones, would be discovered to have made false declarations in some or other or all of the endless forms and documents they had had to fill out, and many would be cornered for not paying income tax, not collecting VAT—or collecting it and not sending it in—or for breaking some of the myriad rules and regulations about terms of service for employees: safe systems of work, paid holidays, insurance, social welfare stamps, and so on.

As for the endless idiotic laws about the care of food and hygiene in shops and restaurants, nobody could possibly comply with even one half of them. Here was another area where the Yoruba—or indeed, any ethnic group that the authorities chose to persecute—would be totally vulnerable. And what about the rules for slaughtering? What were you meant to do in Dublin if you wanted to slaughter a dog for the table? Don't even ask, the rubrics would be so utterly ridiculous! What is actually done is that you take the hound down an alley and hit him on the head with a mallet. What could be more humane? The dog never even knows what hit him.

And what about squirrels? There weren't too many of them around. But a good huntsman could get them in the public parks, as well as some very nice duck—and even deer. The trick with squirrels was to injure them enough to capture them, but to keep them alive: that way the meat stayed fresh until you were ready to eat it. No need to mess with fridges and freezers. This was the kind of thing that the Irish went ballistic about: a hangover, no doubt, from their colonial past, the British being notorious for their lunatic attitudes to animals. The only animal you were allowed to kill with savage cruelty was the only one that you shouldn't want to kill at all, because you cannot eat it: the fox! How much more boneheaded than that can you get?

All of these plagues of investigation and interference were about to descend on the heads of Dublin's Yoruba. Innocent and guilty alike would suffer major hassle and droves of them would probably be expelled. Fat Isaac did not care about that. He was neither Yoruba nor Igbo, nor even from Gboko as he claimed, still less a chief. His mother had been from Shendam in Plateau State. Neither she nor he had any idea who his father was, the coupling necessary to produce Isaac having been the subject of a very temporary and strictly business arrangement requiring no paperwork and lasting less than seven minutes. He had few if any loyalties.

What Isaac did care about was his own skin. Never before in his precarious existence had he been so firmly wedged between a rock and a hard place. If, on the one hand, the Ogboni *had* killed Shad—and it was not a foolish suggestion to say that they might have—they would have it in for Isaac for having said so. If, on the other hand, the Ogboni had *not* killed Shad—they, and the Yoruba more generally, would be just as displeased about his incriminatory words.

If Fat Isaac, like Jude, was having bad dreams, they were not about sex, but about how very much excess flesh he had on either leg for scraping off.

Pita was experiencing all the hardships and hazards of a secret agent's life behind enemy lines. His objective was to stay as close as he could to the doorway into which he had seen Shad disappear with the big, black-haired man on the night when he had been captured and killed. This was indeed the pedestrian entrance to a multistory parking lot. His hope was that, if the black-haired man had used this parking lot before, he might use it again. If he did, Pita would be there to follow him, to get the registration number of his car, to find out who he was—even if he had to jump on top of him and beat him up with his little fists. The problem was that, small as he was, his unrelenting presence in the same place was inescapably conspicuous. The very fact that he was so small, and black, made him even more noticeable.

If this were Moore Street, he could have got some little job with one of the stallholders and melted into the already largely African scenery. But this was Temple Bar. The social welfare and child-protection people would have landed like D-day on the beaches if somebody his size and apparent age had attempted to make himself useful in this fashionably unfashionable area. The fact that he was black would have redoubled their genuine concern and zeal.

At first it was presumed by the restaurateurs and shopkeepers that he was there to pick pockets, to beg, or to shoplift. He did none of those things and was observed over long periods *not* doing them. He was accosted three times in a week by men who took him for a male prostitute. Fortunately, he did not understand their propositions, and they cannot have made much of his replies, which varied from "Happy Christmas" to "and also with you," which is what you said in church to adults who mysteriously wanted to shake your hand. To some people who did ask him directly what he was doing he replied, "I wait." He never said what he was waiting for. He could not find the diplomatic formulas to say, "I am waiting for the black-headed bastard who murdered my friend." So he just said, "I wait."

It was tiring work, standing around all day. He was cold, and often went to bed hungry because he had not been there when the cooking pots of Little Africa were simmering. But his resolve to see this thing through never wavered. Africans know how to wait. They do it for hours, days, weeks, years, uncomplainingly, without resentment or anger. Africa is one enormous school of patience. Not resignation, patience. To be resigned is to have abandoned hope: to be patient is to retain hope intact—and to wait. The whole of Africa has been waiting patiently for centuries for a day that will surely dawn.

In the second week, Pita got a lucky break. He arrived to find that a builder had broken in a shopfront and installed a Dumpster in a boutique almost opposite the entrance to the parking lot. The Dumpster was empty and seemed destined to remain so indefinitely because, as is an Irish custom, nothing further was seen of the builder for several weeks to come. Pita was over the top in a trice and into the belly of the whale. It was to be for him what the ruined elephant of the Bastille had been for Gavroche in the readable, if not the musical version, of *Les Misérables:* observation post, headquarters, and mission control. He quickly piled in bales of insulation, thoughtfully left behind by the absconded builder, and soon had a comfortable platform at one end of the Dumpster, where he could sit or even lie, keep warm, and see without being seen.

The only inconvenience was that ecologically minded passersby tended to throw their unwanted goods in on top of him. Papers and packets didn't matter, but lighted cigarettes, cans, and especially bottles did. On the other hand, he sometimes got things he could eat—if he closed his eyes.

One evening toward dusk, just before he knocked off for the day, and after hearing some mysterious scuffling noises behind the Dumpster that he had failed to understand, he was hit in the face by an oozing condom. He knew that white boys used these things when romancing girls, presumably to keep themselves warm in a cold climate. The only other thing he knew about them was the notorious dictum of Fela, the great Nigerian pop singer: "Condom no good for fuck," which had set the safe sex movement in Nigeria back by several years. He scooped the thing off himself quickly with a closed fist and wiped his face thoroughly on his sweater, disgusted without quite knowing why.

Ten days after Jude's visit to Mrs. Finnerty, a black driver from her husband's business dropped off a package at Shad's Place— Jude had no plans to change that name, ever. The driver said the package was from Mrs. Finnerty. It was peak hour in the evening. Jude and his staff were run off their feet. In an instant, priorities did a somersault. They stopped cooking, serving, and washing dishes. The diners stopped eating. Everybody came over to form a circle around him. They knew what it was.

With trembling fingers he cut the string and removed layers of brown paper and bubble sheeting, uncovering two unbelievably beautiful paintings of Shad. They were identical to the point that, though he knew one had to be an original and the other a copy, he was unable to say which was which. They were big, almost two foot square, strongly mounted and sturdily framed behind glass in dusty brown wood frames that set off the portraits to perfection. Shad, head and shoulders, three-quarter face, was smiling, the dazzling whiteness of his teeth, and of his eyes around their smoldering pupils, suffusing the unblemished skin of his radiantly black face with brilliant light.

They propped the two pictures up on the counter, several feet from each other so that as many people as possible could inspect them closely. If Jude was crying with recognition and joy, he was by no means alone; there was hardly a dry eye in the restaurant. The word went out. People came in off the street and from the snooker hall next door. Tunde, the Yoruba proprietor, stood before the portraits, his eyes glistening. "Shadrack Nwachukwu Okafor, my brother and my friend, friend and brother of all of us here, I give you a new Yoruba title. You shall be called Obawole."

There were approving cries of "*E-he!*" from those who understood. Margot asked:

"What does it mean, Tunde?"

"It means, 'The Prince has come home!'"

For the rest of the evening, there were no more cooks, servers, or customers. Everybody cooked, everybody ate, and everybody washed the dishes. When at a late hour Fat Isaac found himself drying cutlery that Tunde Akintole was washing, he felt his life expectancy increasing by multiples. As they were leaving, people threw money on the counter, one or two even pressing banknotes against Jude's forehead, a traditional gesture of celebration and congratulation.

When they had all gone, Jude and Margot were sitting, still looking at one of the portraits and talking. Jude had decided that one picture would remain always on the restaurant wall. The other he would send back to his mother, or even bring it himself if he could ever get the opportunity and the money to do so. Suddenly, he said:

"Margot, do you remember the evening of the burial, when you found the Blessed Cyprian Tansi chaplet, the rosary beads, on the floor of the funeral car?"

"I do, of course. Why?"

"It was broken, wasn't it, the chaplet?"

She looked at him, astonished.

"It was, yes. One of the links had opened, so it was hanging like a string. I just pressed it closed again between my finger and thumb. But how did you know that it was broken?"

Jude continued looking at the portrait and did not answer.

Molly only heard of Jim Quilligan's departure for Nigeria the same day as he left. He was so busy getting vaccinated against every known disease, collecting his visa, getting briefed on the child-trafficking conference, and arranging a few family affairs that he only managed a few words with her on the telephone and never met up with her face to face. He knew she would be miffed, and she was.

Molly felt that she had a better claim than Quilligan to replace Sheila Hegarty at the child-trafficking meeting. The great majority of children being exploited were girls and a woman would certainly be better able to understand the problems they were facing. She was also actively interested and highly motivated since her meeting with Pita, the orphan *pickin*. She would have loved to learn more about the question and, hopefully, to make a contribution toward solutions. What did Jim Quilligan know about it? Even allowing that he was certainly a nice man and a good husband and father, did he really care? Molly got quite hot about it talking to Jan-Hein.

"Isn't that typical Garda expediency? They are only interested in their flaming cutbacks. It is gross. They are using United Nations money meant for children to finance a routine murder hunt."

Jan-Hein was tempted to ask whether she would say the same thing if the Garda authorities had sent her instead of Quilligan. He decided prudently that such nerdish sweet reason could come later. Meanwhile she needed to off-load some more steam.

"Jan-Hein, you and I are the ones who cracked the code on the Ogboni thing. Do you remember? We sat up all night at that bloody computer. Do you think it would have ever entered Jim's thick head to go online? Or Denis? That poor man thinks a computer is somebody who takes the bus to work every morning. We are the ones who should be going to Africa!"

Jan-Hein cocked his head sideways, pulled a funny face, and smiled. "Well, you bastard!" she exclaimed, getting the message.

Then she laughed. He took her in his arms.

"You'll feel better about it tomorrow."

"I suppose so. To be fair, I don't think Jim—or indeed, Denis—would have done this out of any bad motive, or to do me down."

"Sweetheart, from what we hear, Nigeria, or a lot of African countries, would be difficult terrain for a woman—I don't mean for the UN thing, which will be international and entirely gender okay. But for you to be going around asking tribal chiefs and priests of the river to tell you their dark secrets—it just wouldn't work."

"Huh! Well, I wouldn't bother asking them anything."

"No? So what would you do?"

"I'd ask their wives. I bet you, they'd tell me things that Quilligan won't hear."

"I hadn't thought of that. It is very interesting and probably true. But I'll bet you another thing."

"What's that?"

"That Jim Quilligan is not having the time of his life."

If not perhaps having the time of his life, Quilligan was not doing too badly. Cruising comfortably at several hundred miles an hour, six or seven miles above the Sahara, he was enjoying a preprandial gin-and-tonic and looking forward to a good meal. A simple man at heart, Jim had never outgrown the pleasant curiosity of wondering what would be in all those cute little plastic boxes *this* time. Nor was he shy about asking for second helpings, which delighted the flight attendants: it meant that one person at least appreciated their exquisite reheating.

Murtala Muhammed Airport in Lagos is as modern as any in the world. The air-conditioning in the baggage retrieval hall is inadequate, and one does hear stories about what goes on or doesn't go on in air-traffic control, but the Lagos experience does not really begin until you cross the threshold into the great outdoors.

If it was already noticeably sultry when Quilligan stepped out on the tarmac from his plane at six o'clock in the morning, when he emerged again from the terminal building an hour later, the damp heat of the rainy season hit him in the face like the aftershock from some cosmic disaster. Within two minutes, his large frame was drenched with sweat from top to bottom.

He found himself standing with two cases and a laptop in a sort of paddock, like one cow among many in a cattle mart. All around, pressed against the paddock barrier, were hordes of prospective buyers and sellers. Quilligan felt sure that *he* was the white elephant they were all intent on marketing.

The two exits from this corral were controlled by burly policemen equipped with fearsome whips with which they energetically walloped any eager entrepreneur who stepped an inch over some notional line, hoping to be first to meet, and greet, and fleece the culture shell-shocked traveler from Europe. But once he himself had traversed the magic line between the whips and the whirlpool, Quilligan was in the fallen world of private enterprise—and how!

Four boys instantly grabbed his suitcases, as he clutched the laptop to his breast like a first-born suckling child. They were all shouting cheerfully, "This way, master! This way!" But as each boy was pulling in a different direction, the situation was both urgent and perplexing. It seemed likely that his suitcases would imminently disappear in at least two opposite directions, and that he would be left wondering which one to follow, and which one he could best survive without.

Meanwhile, three mellifluous drivers were proposing three different taxis "for drop," which means that he would have the vehicle to himself and would not have to share it with half the population of Lagos. With eight other people in a taxi, built for maximum five, and without air-conditioning, things were bound to get sticky in the tropics. One cannot sit idly by ignoring anything that happens in that taxi. In the literal, physical, and cosmic sense, it is a continuum and everyone is part of everything. If, for instance, the large lady beside you decides to breast-feed her infant, you cannot avoid personal involvement of the most intimate kind. You may even get breakfast.

On the other hand, "strength in numbers" is part of our received wisdom. In a taxi with eight other people—and throw in a driver—one is less likely to get robbed, raped, or murdered. The real danger, Quilligan had been warned, is one of those gangs of armed cutthroats who lie in wait a mile down the road until tipped off by scouts at the airport equipped with sharp eyes and cellphones. Minutes later, they swarm out and pounce on the designated taxi with its hand-picked foreigner, just in from Europe or the U.S., festooned with cameras and expensive-looking luggage.

The next circle of the inferno at the airport was a wave of gruesomely handicapped people holding up stumps of arms and legs, faces half eaten away, many of them blind, all clamoring their pathetic pleadings. These are burned-out lepers or victims of polio, or war, of prison, of road accidents, fires and explosions in oil pipes from which they or others were trying to steal the contents, of disasters of so many other kinds. It is always men that one sees. What happens to handicapped women?

While Quilligan was trying to decide what to do about all these dilemmas, he heard a distinctly Cork accent in his ear.

"Jim Quilligan, is it?"

He turned eagerly to find a handsome, middle-aged priest standing beside him. He was dressed in a white soutane and shoulder cape, like the pope, and was smiling. "You are welcome. I am Dick Dorr. I had an e-mail from your Superintendent Lennon's Uncle Mike to say that you were coming. Well, I happened to be in Lagos, and I am going back to Benin today. Would you like to come with me?"

Would he what?!

The priest was driving a white VW beetle. Quilligan had not seen one in years. Somebody told him later that they were still being made in Brazil. Like many other cars, they were also coming in, secondhand, from Europe, where the dealers were eager to get them out of the country so that their own customers would have to buy new. By far the most popular car in Nigeria, he learned, was the French Peugeot. Father Dick explained why:

"They collared the market early. Left-hand steering wheel: we drive on the right—in theory anyhow—good spare parts availability, and, most important, the high sump, essential if you don't want to leave your undercarriage behind in a pothole. The roads look okay now. By the end of rainy season, this place can look like the moon."

They drove to a convent near the airport where they had breakfast and Quilligan took the opportunity to have a shower. He fished his lightest clothes out of a suitcase and put them on. These might have been cool at the North Pole, but not in Lagos, which is practically on the equator.

They were on the road for Benin City before 9:00 A.M. The car had no air-conditioning but once they got moving on the open road, with all windows open, it was quite comfortable. Still, the first forty minutes, until they had cleared the city, were mercilessly hot and dusty. The traffic was dense and, to European eyes, chaotic. The one rule of the road seemed to be survival of the quickest, but there was no road rage, only a cheery wave if the other guy got there before you. When you saw a gap, you made for it, no matter whose side of the road it was on. The drivers were remarkably skillful in their anarchy, all the more so, Father Dick explained, as many of them probably had no brakes worth talking of.

Even in the traffic jams, there was so much happening. Policemen with whips, and the special traffic cops in yellow shirts, known to everyone as Yellow Fever, who did manage amazingly to keep things moving. There was every sort of vehicle around them: private cars, buses, enormous wagons belching lethal clouds of black diesel fumes into the windows of cars jammed up tight behind them. Quilligan remembered guiltily that this was how, in the days of his youth, they used to dispose of unwanted puppies and kittens: in a cardboard box hooked up to a diesel exhaust. Those massacred little animals were getting some sort of poetic justice this morning.

Some of the drivers, seeing Dick's white soutane, would shout cheerful greetings—"Fadda!"—as they maneuvered nonetheless skillfully to cut in ahead of him. One, who obviously did not think much of his driving skills, shouted good-naturedly, "Fadda, get yourself a driver!"

Twice, boys passing by Quilligan's open window looked at him shyly and called, "Onyatcha!"

He asked Father Dick what this meant. The priest laughed. "It just means 'white man'! It is a greeting, and perhaps an exorcism."

"An exorcism! You mean that white men are demons?"

"Black people could hardly be blamed for thinking that sometimes they are. Not so?"

In and out, between and around the traffic, there swarmed an army of traders, mostly young men and boys, though there were also girls and older women. Carrying their wares on great round trays balanced on their heads, these traders wove their way effortlessly through all the confusion of stationary, then suddenly moving transports. Such a staggering variety of merchandise was on offer: drinking water in plastic pouches, ground nuts wrapped in cones, fruit, biscuits, toilet rolls, toilet seats, and lavatory brushes. There were maps, towels, watches, books, shirts, underwear, Biros, toys, penknives, suitcases, handbags, beauty aids of every description, and religious pictures—Italianate horrors without a trace of Africa in them.

"That's what they want," said the priest, "Holy Mary with blue eyes, golden hair, and advanced anemia, and Baby Jesus with rosy lips, more blue eyes, and dimples. I tried to put a black madonna and child into my church and they complained of me to the bishop! It's tragic. They have such wonderful artists of their own—and they pass them up for this trash."

CHAPTER EIGHT

PITA HAD TO MEET HIS TUTOR, PEGGY BREEN, THREE mornings a week at nine o'clock. It would not do to miss that rendezvous. First, because he enjoyed the sessions and felt that he was learning a lot, which he was. Peggy was delighted with his progress, though she did think that he seemed tired recently and sometimes did not have his assignments ready. Second, Pita was reluctant to miss classes because he was in love with Peggy, although he still intended to marry Margot. And third, he came because he knew that if he started missing classes, the child welfare people would want to know why. They would soon discover his surveillance post south of the river and would almost certainly close it down. They were so protective—which was nice most of the time: it made him feel special—but it could also be a nuisance, like, at first, when they made him wear "cover-shoe" instead of the comfortable flip-flops he was used to.

Three days a week, therefore, because of the tutorials, Pita did not get to his Dumpster lookout until midmorning. On those days he ran the whole way to Temple Bar straight after his class, convinced that he had just missed his quarry by not being there earlier. When, one Wednesday, three weeks after he had started his vigil, his class was canceled because Peggy had to bury her granny, Pita took it as a sign from heaven that today was the day when his patience would at last be rewarded. He ran to Temple Bar even faster than usual and scrambled up into his crow's nest, his heart pounding with excitement. His intuition was well-founded.

He was barely installed on his platform when he saw the man. His clothes were different but it was the same man, he had no doubt. Black hair slicked back with palm oil or whatever, big, though perhaps not quite as big as the giant policeman with the strange name. The man was walking up the street directly toward Pita's position. If the child had a rifle, or indeed his bow and arrow, he could have shot him straight between the eyeballs: blue eyeballs, he noted. The man stopped to light a cigarette. He was now so close that Pita could see the ring on his finger and the heavy gold watch on his wrist.

Pita started to scramble down from his perch, ready to fall in behind his quarry and follow. Just as the man passed beneath him, he tossed his empty cigarette packet up into the Dumpster. A hard corner of the packet caught the child straight in the eye, crushing two of his long eyelashes back against the pupil. Sudden agony and blindness. Taken totally by surprise, Pita toppled the rest of the way to the floor of his refuge, gashing his knee against the rough edge of some debris there before him. Dazed and shocked, sobbing with sudden pain, one small fist pressed against his damaged eye, the other hand clutching his knee, he still managed to drag himself up by the elbows and over the edge of his dugout. He *must* follow that man. Then he lost balance and fell in a heap into the street.

Passers-by stood back in shocked amazement at this sudden apparition, then closed around him, wanting to help an obviously

hurt and distressed child. Still holding his eye with one hand—
the knee was expendable—he tried to push his way with the
other hand past these gathering Good Samaritans. Hobbling on
his injured leg, he strained every muscle to escape, to run, to
catch up with Shad's murderer, to capture him or, at least, that
much at least—oh merciful God—to see where the monster was
going!

It was hopeless. The more frantic he became, the tighter they
held him protectively. And, as for seeing, how could he see anything, with one eye closed behind his tightly clenched fist, and
the other blinded by tears of pain and frustration?

They took him into a nearby pharmacy. There they coaxed his eye
open, got the lashes out, cleaned it, put in soothing drops, and
made sure that there was no serious lesion. The knee might have
needed stitches: on balance, they thought not. They cleaned it
well, slapped on disinfectant and a firm bandage. The pharmacist
penned a note, "for your mummy," advising that he should have a
tetanus injection. He did not feel entitled to make that decision
himself.

They were puzzled by this child. That a youngster should go
playing on a building site did not surprise anyone, that he should
fall and hurt himself was also on the cards. What they did not understand was his excessive distress. Had somebody beaten him?
Was there something more sinister behind this banal event? He
barely spoke. He did not seem to understand their questions.
While two kind people, who had stayed with him in the pharmacy, were discussing with the manager what best to do next,
Pita slipped behind their backs and escaped into the street.

He hobbled back across the river, a one-man defeated army,

deeply dejected. Napoleon on his way back from Moscow could not have felt more deflated. He had been sure, he *knew* that he would find that man someday, however long it might take. And when, by God's grace, he *did* find him, what had he done? He had acted like a small boy, worse, like a clumsy, brainless fool, like a village idiot on market day who drinks himself stupid on palm wine!

He reproached himself mercilessly: those were minor injuries. He should have ignored his pain. He should have gone straight after that man and caught him. He should have shouted to all those people, "Murderer! Murderer! Stop am o!" He should have told them to get the police, to jump on the man and hold him. Instead of which—the shame of it—he had let them drag him away to fuss about his trivial injuries. The gods had given him the chance that he had prayed for, and fasted for, gone without sleep for, and waited and waited for. And he had wasted that chance for his own small comfort! He had not been worthy of it. He had failed Shad. His tears began to flow again.

He went home in a zigzag way, not wishing to pass through streets where he would be recognized, and where people, seeing the state he was in, would torture him with unwanted questions and undeserved kisses. Rounding the corner into Parnell Street, he bumped straight into Margot coming back from some shopping. She saw in one glance the extent of his disarray.

"Pita, what happened? Sweetheart, what is wrong with you?"

He gritted his teeth and stopped breathing. He held good for four seconds. Then the floodgates opened. He fell into her arms weeping uncontrollably.

Margot had brought Pita back to the restaurant and called Jude. They sat him down at one of the tables in the dining room. Gently, a few words at a time, they winkled the whole story out of him. When it was finished, they exchanged glances of amazement. They would talk about it between themselves later, many times: the unselfishness of the child, his patience, his loyalty to Shad, and his sheer courage. They were both profoundly moved. Margot had done all the things that only a woman can do in such situations. She had held the child close. She had stroked his head and face, she had hugged him and kissed him. Jude knew now what he had to do.

"Stand, Pita, come!"

They stood out in the center of the floor facing each other. Jude held up his forearm, his hand sideways to his face. The boy did likewise. They locked fingers, then unlocked again, turned their hands around, locked again, turned again, locked again, several times. Pita's face was suddenly radiant. This was the warrior's salute, the way the noble and fearless young men greet and acknowledge each other. His heart sang. Nobody had ever given him this greeting before. This was his first time. No word was spoken because no word was needed. The gesture said it all:

You are a man, you are my brother and my equal. I affirm you, I applaud you. You are brave and good. You are a true warrior. You would die for me and for Shad, and I would die for you.

After that, if the warrior was still disappointed that the murderer had gotten away, his heart was peaceful and full of joy. After lunch in the restaurant, when he ate what was probably his first proper meal in a month, he lay down on a bench behind the counter and went fast asleep. He slept until late afternoon. Everybody tiptoed around him.

By the time Pita woke up, Jude had thought of something important.

"Pita, what did you say this man throw at you?"

"He throw his *this-thing* into the *something*."

Jude was Igbo by tribe, Pita was Ijaw. Each spoke one out of several hundred languages currently spoken in Nigeria. Their only possible means of communication was English, the lingua franca and the first official language of the country. Jude's English was improving, in the sense of becoming more comprehensible to an English person. Pita's was still closer to pidgin which has other roots as well as English, such as Portuguese, and a more rudimentary syntax. Whereas Jude, too, might have used the indefinite nouns (the) "something" and (his) "this-thing," which are current in Nigerian English, he would hardly have put the two in the same sentence. Pita's pidgin, as spoken in the Delta, would translate into Dublin pidgin, as spoken in the Liberties, as: "He thrun his gadget into the yoke," which would be just as incomprehensible for an Oxford don.

"Yes, Pita, but what was his 'this-thing'?"

"Aha! It is box for cigarettes."

"A cigarette pack?"

"Yes, that one."

"Is it still there, in the builder's 'something'?"

"Yes now."

"Did you touch it?"

"No, it touch me!"

"Pita, we must go and get this one."

"Aha! For am make strong juju?"

"No, for fingerprints."

"What is fingerprints?"

"Come, show me. I will explain as we go."

He took a small plastic bag to collect the cigarette box, as he had seen the police do it on television. Then they set off, back toward the river, walking, talking, and holding hands. In Nigeria, it is not proper for a young man to hold hands with a young woman in public, but for young men to hold hands in the street is the most normal thing in the world.

Napoleon rejoiced to hold hands with his warrior brother and to turn the battle back so soon toward Moscow.

The UN conference was being held at the Catholic Archdiocesan Conference Center on Airport Road. Some of the last-minute delegates, including Quilligan, were being accommodated in a smaller conference center run by the medical missionaries a few miles away across town.

The inspector's chief motive for being in Nigeria was to pursue the murder inquiry on which he was engaged. He was nonetheless determined that, chronologically, this first priority would become second. For the duration of the Child Protection Conference, Shad's case could, should, and would have to wait.

The most powerfully moving and unforgettable episode during the four days was the personal testimony of four young women who stood up and told their stories with devastating simplicity and directness. Two of the women were African, one Eastern European, and one from an Arab country. It was essentially the same story, not just for the four, but for countless others for whom they spoke. Born into poor families or orphaned, frequently by the death of parents with AIDS, they were dispatched, often with a group of other girls, almost always to a country different from the one they had been told in advance, under the pretext of receiving a good education, with the prospect of becoming nurses, teachers, even religious sisters, or of marrying wealthy and loving husbands. The reality was heartbreakingly different. These girls, and sometimes boys, were destined for lives of abject misery, as slaves, concubines, or prostitutes.

One of the strong themes of the conference was the relative indifference of the media to the plight of these children. As one Brazilian delegate put it, "Nobody wants to hear about exploitation of kids—unless some priests or nuns can get blamed for it. Yeah, that's news, all right—even if it happened fifty years ago. But the wider problem, and what is happening out there right *now*—they don't want to know about it!"

Quilligan, who would not have considered himself a pillar of the Church, and moreover was not into giving speeches, found himself on his feet.

"I know that, in my own country, whatever way this thing has been handled, most people believe that child abuse is mostly done by priests and that big percentages of priests are child abusers. I don't know what the actual percentages are but I do know that they are very small. The opposite impression has been created. I am not defending child abusers: they have done the worst, and they deserve the worst, but . . ."

Quilligan was conscious of uncomfortable stirrings around him. The chairperson cut in to say that what the Irish delegate was saying was not really relevant. The conference was concerned with present and future problems, not with the past.

"Yes, well, I am just saying that if you treat the past like shit, don't be surprised if the present and the future don't work out too well for you."

There were gasps of disapproval on all sides. The simultaneous translators could be seen throwing their arms in the air behind their little glass panels. They had never before been asked to translate "shit." Perhaps the word, not to speak of the reality, did not exist in their beautiful languages.

That evening, Quilligan met one of the British delegates in a bar, a man called Huttingberry, who was somewhat the worse for wear.

"By Jove, Quillikins, how did the *Oirish* ever let you out on your own?"

"Why?"

"Attacking the press like that. There is only one way with the media, don't you know that?"

"Really? What is it?"

"Kiss ass."

"I'd prefer to eat shit, as our African friends say."

"You may have to. Don't you know that you can never win a match against the media? They own the pitch, and they always play downhill and with the wind. Simple as that!"

"I have no quarrel with the media. I have loads of journalist friends."

"Have you then? Well, even your journalist friends have got to earn their living. Except in very few organizations, journalists don't count. Owners count, and editors count. And what they count is money, market figures, and what sells their product."

"And what about the truth?"

"Look, Quillikins, don't be such a bleeding idiot! It is not a question of truth against lies: it is a question of *which* truth you need to go with. Take my word for it, if you can't work it out for yourself. Pedophile priests sell lots more newspapers and earn much more advertising revenue than prissy little articles about retired missionaries tottering around on their walking frames."

"Yes, but doesn't a truth which is only part of the truth become a lie if you keep presenting it as the whole truth?"

"Quillikins, get yourself a life, will you? Listen, do you realize—have you any idea how pissed off they are with you here?"

"Who, the journalists?"

"Nuts. One or two of them are even praising you. It's the handlers who are furious with you, the UN mandarins, who want, who need, and who are determined to get good media support on this thing."

"It's not just me. What about Suarez, the Brazilian guy?"

"He won't even be mentioned. But you will be mentioned, and you won't like what they have to say about you. Don't expect the UN to send in the *blue helmets* to bail you out. They won't. They want results for the kids. That is central, and that is all! If you want to turn this whole circus into a private war to save the ancient druids, you're on your own, Quillikins, you're on your fucking own."

Molly flattened out the crumpled page on her desk. It had been torn from the middle of a child's copybook. The handwriting, in black Biro, and the content were not so much childish as seriously undereducated. There was no punctuation, and the grammar and spelling were very feeble.

I have to tel ye that this hapen'd before there was a body for the creamotorium las yere and her leg was gone and there was

a gra leg sone on instede in its plase I sene it and it was des-
perete an I hav to tel ye btu I'd be kilt an they know.

This communication, unsigned and undated, had been posted in
a cheap envelope without a stamp the previous day at the GPO.
It was addressed to:

The Guards,
Dublin.

The postal authorities had delivered the envelope to Garda headquarters in the Phoenix Park. Whoever opens such imprecisely
addressed missives at headquarters had decided that this one
must have something to do with Shad's case and had forwarded it
by internal Garda courrier to Denis Lennon. He, in turn, had
sent it on to Molly with his own suggested "translation" and an
invitation to come and discuss it when she had had a chance to
think about it. His version was nicely written out in his best
Gothic script.

I have to tell you that this (has) happened before.
There was a body for the Crematorium last year, and her leg
was gone, and there was a gray leg sewn on instead in its place.
I seen it, and it was desperate, and I have to tell you,
but I would be killed if they knew.

Molly went to see Lennon the next day.
"Are we agreed about what the letter says, Molly?"
"Oh, I think so, your translation seems to be spot on."
"Thank you; but what does it mean? 'This has happened be-
fore.' *What* has happened before?"

"I suppose that somebody's leg has been chopped off."

"Perhaps, but it is more complicated than that. It says that this woman's leg was *gone*: it doesn't say how or where it went. We know it is a woman because it says 'her' leg. It continues that 'a gray leg was sewn on instead in its place.' So that gray leg certainly had to be cut off somebody else before it got sewn onto this woman. We don't know whether either, or neither, or both of these people was or were alive or dead when their legs were being chopped off or sewn on."

"Denis, do you think it is possible that Shad's leg, or foot I suppose, could have been grafted onto another person, and is even now walking around Dublin, attached to somebody else?"

"I very much doubt it, if the standard of surgery in sewing on new legs was as basic as the chopping off of the old one and the patching up of the poor donor afterward. The question is: What is this letter writer trying to say? Are we talking about pioneering work in organ transplants, or is it merely a question of post-mortem cosmetics? Because the crematorium was in on the act, the evidence is all burned up, so we don't get a chance to check up and find out."

"We are assuming that this all refers to Shad. I mean, that is what the letter writer seems to be saying, so we try to harmonize all the elements between his case and this case. So what about color, does color come into it? The only color mentioned here is 'gray.' That sounds like a dead leg."

"In less than prime condition. But was it originally a white leg or a black leg?"

"Exactly! That is the question, isn't it?"

"Well, Molly, one thing we are sure of: this person is definitely reporting a wrongdoing, and very probably a murder, and is obviously very fearful about doing so. What can we say about the person who wrote this letter? What kind of a person should we be looking for?"

"I've thought about that. Here is my best guess: middle-aged, a woman, not well educated, and a Dub."

Lennon chuckled, nodding his head admiringly.

"Excellent! I think you are absolutely right, but now tell me why."

"The lack of education is quite obvious."

"Yes, unless it is assumed, to cover the writer's tracks and preserve anonymity."

"Could be, but I doubt it."

"And what about a woman, and a Dub, and a middle-aged one?"

"Look at the expressions used. 'I seen it, and it was desperate, and I'd be kilt.' That is real Ould Dublin Shawlie talk. You could be listening to Biddy Mulligan. Since the free education came in, and the television, the younger people don't talk like that anymore."

"Too true, alas! Molly, you are brilliant. But why middle-aged? We have had the television and the free education for a long time now. Why not an *old* woman?"

"Firstly, there are probably children still around if she can get her hands on a copybook for her sheet of paper."

"She could be a granny."

"She probably is. Dublin grannies of that vintage were often teenage mothers. This woman is probably not old. She seems to be still in employment. 'I would be kilt if they knew'—meaning, if they knew that I was telling you about this. Who are 'they'? Very likely, employers who would not like this information to be made known."

"Because it would reflect badly on them?"

"Yes."

"So what kind of employers would that be?"

"Well, I started with the crematorium. There are two within easy reach of here, Glasnevin and Mount St. Jerome. I went out to Glasnevin and talked to—I think he is the manager or the deputy director, a nice chap—with a good line in gallows humor."

"I'm sure he needs it."

"Well, he was quite categorical. Working in a cemetery or in a crematorium, the one thing you will never see is a dead body."

"Really? One would have thought."

"One would have thought—but no. I think he said it is the law, or a rule. The dear departed must arrive in boxes and be 'processed'—that is the word he used—in boxes, i.e., buried or burned. Under no circumstances may the personnel open a casket."

"Do you mean that the whole coffin goes into the flames?"

"It does. Everything is consumed by fire. A strong magnet is then used to extract any metal that may remain, like dental fillings, surgical implants, bullets from the First World War, whatever, even handles off the more elaborate caskets. All that is left then is bones. That is what you get back in the urn eventually—duly reduced to a convenient . . ."

"Good Lord, how do they . . . ?"

"Don't ask. The important thing is that whoever wrote us this note did not see whatever she saw in the crematorium. Crematorium staff don't see bodies."

"That is very interesting. Here is what the note says: 'There was a body *for* the crematorium.' That does not have to mean a body *coming to* the crematorium: it could mean a body *going to* the crematorium. Where do bodies going to the crematorium come from?"

"From the church, I suppose."

"Well, I don't imagine that the clergy would be opening caskets, either, to give them their due. And before the church?"

"From the funeral home nowadays, or from the hospital, sometimes from a private house. I might ask Mr. Finnerty. He is the nice man who did Shad's funeral for free."

"By the time he got his hands on poor Shad, the damage had been done."

"Of course, but he would know about what goes on in funeral homes and what somebody could or could not see. He might even be able to narrow the field down for us, so that we could track our pen friend. She could easily be a cleaning woman, or something like that, in one of the Dublin funeral homes."

"Well done, Molly! Jim will be thrilled—especially if the trail leads eventually to his secret society friends. What's this you call them?"

"Ogboni?"

"Ogboni, that's the lads."

CHAPTER NINE

JIM QUILLIGAN HAD JUST BEEN READING WHAT ONE IRISH newspaper, and two British newspapers masquerading as Irish newspapers, had been saying about him. His wife had faxed the cuttings out to him with cheerful assurances of her own undying love.

The chosen high ground was a righteously indignant complaint about how shameful it was for Ireland, and how embarrassing for the United Nations, that the Irish Police authorities had sent to Benin City, as delegate to an international conference for the protection of children, a redneck oaf who did not know the first thing about the difficult, delicate, and urgent problems that the conference was trying so hard to resolve.

Incredibly, the reports continued, it now seemed that this officer, although fully funded by the United Nations, was really in Nigeria in connection with a totally unrelated police inquiry. His only contribution to the Benin conference had been to complain bitterly about how rigorously the Irish media had pursued priests guilty of abusing children.

There were demands for the Garda commissioner to make a statement about this disgraceful incident.

Quilligan was named in all three reports, one newspaper even claiming that it had been able to "discover" his identity, as if the name Quilligan was somebody's guilty secret. It was deftly added, in the same newspaper, that Inspector Quilligan's family had "eventually settled in West Limerick some years ago." No Irish reader would have difficulty deciphering what that was meant to mean: This guy is a tinker, so what do you expect?

Quilligan knew that no Irish newspaper had a reporter at the conference. As he said to Father Dick that evening:

"I don't know whose copy they are taking, but I sure as hell know where the whore is coming from."

"I note with interest," Father Dick commented, "that apart from groaning at your deplorable behavior, they don't say one single, solitary word about what *else* this major world conference has been doing for the last week. That shows how much they really care."

"You're damn right."

"So you have succeeded in your devilish plan to scupper the whole thing, to the advantage of us ravening pedophile priests. Thanks, pal!"

"Oh shit, it is so frustrating! Shut up anyhow, and get me another beer." Quilligan had soon decided that he had never been anywhere in the world where chilled beer tasted more delicious.

The evening the conference had ended, Dick Dorr collected Jim Quilligan and drove him to his parish house at Agbor, halfway between Benin City and Onitsha, where he hoped to visit Jude's family the next day. After most of a week in the country, he was getting used to the idea that the sun shot up at 6:00 A.M. every morning and disappeared even more suddenly at 6:00 P.M. each evening, giving twelve hours of light and twelve hours of darkness year round. It was no surprise, therefore, that they left Benin in broad daylight, and arrived forty minutes later at Agbor in total darkness.

The evening was deliciously cool. The two men sat out on an open verandah after supper, sipping cold beer and listening to the repertoire of countless millions of insects. Dick professed not to hear them anymore, after all these years in the tropics, at least until somebody mentioned them. He was also largely immune to their bloodthirsty onslaughts, whereas Quilligan had to put on socks to discourage sand flies and paint his face and arms with something disgusting to repel mosquitoes.

"Virgin blood, Jim; they love it. After a few months they won't even look at you."

Quilligan peppered the priest with questions about all aspects of African life. Dick confirmed that there was virtually no big game left except in the reservations and on isolated stretches of the big rivers.

"Smaller stuff, yes: antelope, grass cutters, bush rabbits. Plenty of snakes, of course, and scorpions. Be sure to look under your pillow."

"You're not serious!"

"I am perfectly serious. Snakes are shy creatures and they will do you no harm, unless you stand on one or give him a fright. The spitting cobra is the only one around here that is a bit malicious. He can get you in the eye at five yards."

"Holy God, and what am I meant to do?"

"Spit first! When he sees your glob in midair, he gets discouraged. Of course, your throat will probably go dry, from the fright, and you won't have anything to spit with."

"Come off it, Dick, you are pulling my leg!"

"Of course, the other way is to hold your watch up over your nose and close your eyes tight."

"What good would that do?"

"Then he thinks that you're a cyclops, and that the watch is your eye. He'll spit at that instead."

"You're a fierce liar, padre; I don't know what to believe! But, come here to me now—and treat this one seriously. What about juju and witchcraft, and pagan worship, and all that stuff? That's what I really came here to find out about. Is this what killed young Shad?"

"Well, to begin with, we avoid words like 'pagan' and 'witch doctor' nowadays. They are disrespectful to a whole culture and way of life. We say 'traditional,' traditional religion, traditional medicine, so on. There is a lot of fear and superstition out there, certainly, and that cannot be good, but there is also a lot of genuine spirituality, Jim, and wisdom, too. Take herbal medicine, for instance: the good native doctors are marvelous."

"But there is a demonic side, too, isn't there?"

"Yes, sometimes. I have seen some frightening things. But, believe me, you don't have to come to Africa for that. The more secularized Europe becomes, the more people are lapsing back into superstition, and the more vulnerable they become to the satanic."

"Well, do you think that some of this devil stuff might be mixed up in Shad's murder? I mean, the whole bloody thing is so off-the-wall, so weird, compared to any case I have ever been in."

"I think you still mean 'African' every time you say 'devil.'"

"Perhaps I do. It is certainly not any devil I have ever met before; and I have met a few."

The priest nodded sagely several times.

"Next tomorrow—sorry, that is Nigerian for 'the day after tomorrow'—I will bring you to Ekpoma to meet Professor Ogogie. He probably knows more about African devils than any man living. He is also high in the echelons of the Ogboni cult, in which you are so interested. The professor, I must warn you, does not suffer fools gladly—I am sorry to put it so baldly—and he only rarely agrees to this kind of interview. Still, if you are careful how you handle him—especially in relation to Ogboni—I think you may hear what you need to hear."

Delta State, Nigeria, and Inner Dublin, Ireland, are far removed from each other in space, but inseparable in time, sitting, as they do, on more or less the same line of longitude. As two Irishmen sat in Nigeria discussing the Nigerians, two Nigerians sat in Dublin discussing what to do next about the Irish.

"Jude, why you do no bring this cigarette something to the police?"

"Cigarette *box,* Pita," Jude corrected.

"It is all right, cigarette *box.*"

"Because I do not trust the police. Police eat money. You know that. If someone bring them money, the police will lose our cigarette box, and if someone bring them more money, the police will lose you and me out of this country. Alive or dead will not matter."

"Miss Molly is good. She no eat money."

"Yes, but Miss Molly is not the big chief. It is this Quilligan somebody who leads the dance. Do you know that he has gone to Nigeria? For why has he gone? I no know why he has gone. If he asks money from my mother, I will kill him."

"He give me his dinner one time."

"He is friendly on the surface, but he is in league with this Finnerty people. He is the one who bring the news that Mr. Finnerty will pay for Shad's funeral. Why will he pay? And why does Quilligan bring this news? Pita, I am not happy about Shad and this Finnerty people. They have capture his *chi*."

"*Chi?*"

"*Chi*, that is Igbo, that is his spirit, his soul. Mrs. Finnerty take his body, and inside his body is his *chi*."

"*Eeh!* You mean she fuck with him?"

"No! Shad never romance this woman. And, Pita, do not use this 'fuck' word. It is not polite in Dublin."

The boy laughed outright.

"Jude, you talk joke! The area boys in Dublin is saying 'fuck-fuck' everytime. Like I say 'something' and 'this-thing,' they say this 'fuck' thing *everytime*. They have no much other word in their language."

"All right, but don't let Miss Breen hear you saying it."

"Miss Breen is very clever teacher. She show me how to write this word. I axe her one time."

"*Ask*, not axe," Jude corrected. It was his turn to laugh. He threw his eyes to heaven.

"Pita, you go corrupt this whole city! But listen, seriously. The police eat money, and I don't like this Finnerty people. Madame Finnerty have make slave of Shad's *chi*, and then he go die. Her husband bury his body. Now she give me back his *chi* in his picture—when it is too late."

"Jude, I don't think the Irish police eat money. And are you sure-sure that this Finnerty people do bad thing for Shad?"

"I know it, Pita."

"How do you know it, Jude?"

"My ancestors is telling me, in a too horrible dream."

"Tell me this dream."

"Pita, I cannot tell you this one."

"Am I not your brother?"

"Yes, Pita, I love you too much, as my brother; but this dream is too terrible. You would not understand, and I would not have the words to tell you."

"It is all right, Jude. I believe you."

They both laughed. Jude had really found a brother in Pita. His speech was sometimes childlike and comical, but his heart was good and his head wise beyond his years. Besides, he had proved his courage and his fierce loyalty. Jude found it helped him to talk to Pita. He also knew that Pita needed this.

In Africa, a boy can go and sit in the window and listen to the men's palaver. This is how he learns to listen attentively, to keep his mouth shut, and not to repeat what he has heard. Then, as he listens, the boy learns how to make wise judgments himself, how to speak well and persuade other people, using many apt proverbs and telling stories to illustrate his arguments. The boy also learns good manners, how to respect elders, but also how to disagree with them, firmly but very politely, when his heart says that he must. Jude was happy to make up some of all this for the little orphan.

"Anyhow, Pita, there is more than my dreams. There is the chaplet."

He opened his shirt and showed the boy the Blessed Cyprian Tansi rosary beads around his neck, the crucifix resting on his chest.

"Aha! I know this one. Shad told me how you two got them on that holy day. He loved his chaplet too much."

"Do you know that when his body was found, his chaplet was gone vanish?"

"Ah no!"

"I give him my very own one in his coffin, to bury with him. Then, that very same day, during the entertainment, Margot find this one under the seat of the big black funeral car we have for that day."

Jude lifted the chaplet over his head, kissed it, and held it out in his hands.

"Look, Pita, this is not my chaplet. My chaplet is in the grave with Shad. This is Shad's chaplet."

"You mean it!"

"I mean it. Look here, the picture of Pope John Paul has small crack. That is Shad's one. He showed me this thing his very self when it happened."

"So that means somebody thieved Shad's own chaplet when he is living, and let it fall in the car after he is dead. Who could that be?"

"Aha! I ask myself that question many times—until at last I understand. Pita, nobody have thieved Shad's chaplet. It fall off his own neck when he is lying on the floor of that very same car, still alive but already half-dead because that is the very car they use to drive him into the lonely mountains after they have cut off his foot."

"*Eeeeeh!*"

"Yes now! I asked Madame Margot. She tell me that the chaplet was broken open in one place when she find it. She repair it easily with her hand. But that is how it fell to the floor in that car from Shad's own neck. Perhaps he is fighting . . . but he is dying. They drag him out of the car, and the chaplet lie there until Margot find it. You see now why I do not trust this policeman and why I don't trust this Finnerty people. They are all the same bundle of sticks with themselves."

"What will you do, Jude?"

"I will fight them."

The boy was on his feet.

"I will fight them, too!"

Mr. Patrick Finnerty owned four funeral homes strategically placed around the Dublin suburbs, two north of the river, and two on the south. The business had been started by his grandfather as an old-style undertaker's, very much of the kind where Oliver Twist's mournful expression secured him his first employment. They sized up corpses with a tape measure and put them in boxes, using a little persuasion to overcome any slight disproportion between physical volume and available containers. They transported these boxes to churches, and from there to cemeteries, or to "graveyards," as the Irish like to call them. That was about the range of services in those days.

Patrick's father had dutifully assisted the founding patriarch and, together with his two brothers, carried on the business when the old gentleman caught a chill in a country churchyard and became, in all senses, his own latest customer. It was in this middle generation that the Finnerty lugubrious expression and graveside manner were perfected. Their highly professional gloom inspired quiet confidence in the bereaved that their burial services would be suitably miserable.

But the old order of things was passing away, and already the winds of change were blowing through the morgues and mortuaries of Ireland. Glimpses were being caught of a better way. Seminal works like Evelyn Waugh's *The Loved One* were being read by the nation's deep thinkers, whilst American films depicting funerals wholly organized by the Mafia—from bullet to bouquet—were beginning to make their influence felt, even among the common people.

Patrick had hoped to be the one that got away. He wanted to study medicine and to become a healer. He had even run away to the United States to take tentative steps in that direction. But, as the only male issue from the three brothers, whose generative capacities had probably been blunted by their professional lugubriousness, he was relentlesly pursued and finally coralled. He was to come home!

Negotiations followed, and Patrick was allowed two further years in the States, in Brooklyn specifically, on condition that he immersed himself, root and branch, shroud and pall, in an indepth study and hands-on familiarization with what the French call *l'affaire du croque-mort*: the corpse-crunching business.

He stayed five years, and returned to Dublin in the early seventies, replete with all the arcane science of the mortician's art. He lost no time in burying the three brothers, replacing them with four funeral homes in well-chosen neighborhoods, convenient to hospitals, cemeteries, churches, and surrounded by healthy hinterlands of unhealthy, well-heeled potential customers.

Patrick knew and provided for everything that could be done about corpses: embalming, refrigeration, apparel, cosmetics, wakes, cremations, burials at sea, and even the retrieval and transportation of loved ones from the most remote and least cooperative regions of the world. He was one of Ireland's very first state-of-the-art funeral directors.

He looked the part, at least when on duty. If he had changed the last letter of his name from y to i, and called himself Finnerti, the illusion would have been total. He seemed cut in the mold of the great Brooklyn/Italian school of undertaker. Large, black suited, with black hair—heavily greased back, black facial stubble—just short of designer consistency, and dark glasses to conceal the lack of emotion, he even had some gold teeth. Molly thought he might be in his middle fifties, or perhaps a bit older. The hair was probably dyed, or it could even be a hairpiece, if you can put gel on a hairpiece.

He received Molly at his flagship premises in Rathgar. She was shown into a thickly carpeted, solemnly furnished room with plenty of dark wood paneling. The curtains were perpetually drawn, and the light dimmed down to cold comfort, like water for washing corpses. She explained that she was part of the team investigating the murder of that Nigerian young man whom Mr. Finnerty had so generously buried at his own expense.

"Ah, yes, poor Shad, was that his name? I didn't really know him, but he modeled a few times for my wife. She was fond of him. We were glad to do the funeral."

"Have you any ideas about what could have happened to him?"

The undertaker raised his eyebrows in surprise, as if she had said something vaguely improper.

"Well, Miss Power, he died. That is the essential thing from our point of view. In a job like this, one has to be fairly pragmatic. I rarely speculate about how my customers come to be here. We do our bit by them: to bury them decently. If there are issues, we must leave it to the pathologists and to the police, to take these matters forward."

"Yes, of course, but I just thought that, as your wife knew the boy, you, or either of you, might have some idea, or at least some interest in what might have happened to him."

Mr. Finnerty sat back in his chair and spread his hands wide on the desk.

"We see so many tragedies in our business that my wife and I have a sort of unwritten rule not to talk about these things. In this case, I think we would both feel that this was one of these horrible African things that, really, we would prefer not to know about."

"Have you not discussed it between yourselves?"

"Perhaps. But, Sergeant, you have hardly come here hoping to discuss what I talk about to my wife."

There was a rather icy silence. Molly took up on a different tack.

"Mr. Finnerty, you could assist me on a detail of funeral procedure. I need to know what happens when a body is being cremated. Is the body taken out of its coffin—"

Finnerty cut her short. "Excuse me, Sergeant. I don't understand. This young man was not cremated."

"I know. I am talking about another case."

"Whose case?"

"I don't have a name at present. My question is a general one. I would be grateful if you could tell me about what usually happens at a cremation. Is the body taken out of its coffin—or does the whole lot go into the furnace? Excuse me, I know that I haven't got the right words to discuss these, er, procedures."

He nodded stiffly, as if to agree with her last remark.

"What happens is that the body is consigned to the cremation chamber suitably enclosed. Why do you ask?"

"It seems somehow extravagant to buy a very costly casket— and then burn it to ashes two days later."

"I see. What is happening increasingly is that people lease a suitable casket—seeing we are using the American word."

"They *lease* it?"

"Yes, like one rents a comfortable car for a long journey. Accordingly, a family will lease an imposing casket for the lying-in-state, or the wake as we say, for the church service, and for the final commendation at the crematorium chapel. Later in the day, the body is reverently moved to a plain receptacle, which serves adequately for the cremation process."

"Where does that switch take place, at the cemetery?"

The undertaker looked at her as if trying to remember who she was.

"No, Miss Power, the body is brought back to the funeral home. The exchange is made there."

"Thank you, Mr. Finnerty, that is very helpful. If I could ask you just one other thing. Have you ever seen another case like Shad's?"

"Sergeant, all our cases are like Shad's. They are all dead, you know."

"Well, of course; but I mean, a case of a black person who has lost a leg. Have you ever seen that before?"

"Sergeant, I have no idea. I have four different funeral parlors. Most of the people we bury I do not see at all. Besides, what with all the horrific road accidents there are nowadays, it is not unusual for someone to emerge minus an arm or a leg, or even their head. My people spend a lot of time trying to give people back something approximately like a face or a limb."

"Do you sew back limbs after accidents?"

"Yes we do, or after the pathologists have finished their explorations. I can assure you, people need also to be put back together after a postmortem—I'll spare you the details."

"Would you ever replace a missing limb—I mean one that was really missing—by using somebody else's limb?"

The undertaker stared at the policewoman as if she had said something really gross.

"What can you possibly mean?"

"Well, I don't understand it myself. We have had a report of a woman who had lost a leg, and that leg had been replaced by another person's leg."

Mr. Finnerty continued to stare coldly.

"Sergeant, is this a joke? What are you talking about? There would never be any need for such a grotesque procedure. If a limb is missing, we can replace it with a shape in plastic material which, covered by a trouser leg, a sock and a shoe, gives a perfectly acceptable result from the cosmetic point of view."

"So whatever happened in that case I mentioned, it certainly didn't happen in a funeral home?"

"Sergeant, I don't believe it happened anywhere. Even advanced surgery has not got as far as leg transplants. I suggest that whoever gave you that report had been either drinking or dreaming."

He added as a sort of afterthought, "The only real challenge in this area is facial reconstruction. There, you cannot fake it. I trained for that in the U.S., Sergeant. The fact is I should have been a surgeon: I work miracles—on dead people, unfortunately.

"As for black people, we see very few of them here in Dublin—I mean, very few dead ones. The black population is still young and vigorous. But I worked a lot with black skin in Brooklyn. Some of my customers were rather prone to violent accidents. Black skin has unique properties, Sergeant. It is a beautiful material. Shiny, smooth, very satiny, very malleable."

He looked up sharply, as if to gauge her reaction before she could hide it, then smiled humorlessly.

"Well, don't let your imagination run away with you, Sergeant. I didn't kill Shad for his pelt—or your other black woman, either."

"What other black woman?"

"The one you mentioned—as having her leg cut off to replace somebody else's. Isn't that what you said?"

"I never said that she was black."

"No? I thought you were talking about something similar to Shad's case, but I cannot claim to have listened very carefully. Now, if I cannot assist you further . . ."

"Pita, this is probably against the law."

"What is?"

"For me to make this something, and for you to use it."

"Uchedike, you are the only one who can do this. I beg. I am no area boy, you know that. I need this thing to protect my brother."

The old man smiled. It was true, Pita was no "area boy," no street hoodlum. The thought of this child wanting to protect Jude was as typical of him as it was touching. What harm could come of it? Besides, it was so long since Uchedike had exercised his skill, he had thought never to do so again. It would make him feel young and useful, for one last time.

"Very well, child. You have a noble soul. I will do this thing for you. It is God's will."

The boy went down on one knee and kissed the old man's hand.

"Mrs. Finnerty, this is Jude. I am ringing you up."

"No need to shout, Jude. I can hear you perfectly well."

"You are so far away."

"Much too far, Jude, for you to make any difference by shouting."

"But . . ."

"Please, Jude, do *not* shout. I hear you better when you talk quietly. Did you like Shad's picture? I thought you would contact me to, well, to say what you thought of it."

"I have never thanked you, I am sorry. My feelings about Shad and your house . . . I do not know how to say them. I like this picture too much. You have given me back Shad's soul. Can I visit your house again?"

"Why?"

"So that I can *feel* the house again, to find why Shad died."

There was a long pause. Then she said, "Jude, nothing bad ever happened to Shad in my house."

"Please, I beg. It is important."

"I am going away, for several months, Jude. It is necessary for my health. Perhaps when I return."

"Could Mr. Finnerty let me in?"

Another long pause. Finally, "Mr. Finnerty does not live here anymore. Good-bye, Jude."

CHAPTER TEN

QUILLIGAN DID NOT KNOW WHAT TO EXPECT AT SHAD'S home, especially as nobody knew that he was coming. He and the missionary stopped at Nnewi and recruited the parish priest, an excellent Father Anamizu, who agreed to accompany them to the Okafor compound. The house was a few miles outside the town, one of three grouped around a pleasant clearing in the bush. The other two, bigger and with more outhouses, were occupied by Shad's two uncles and their families.

To European eyes, a three-room building with mud walls, unglazed windows, a rusting, corrugated iron roof, and very little furniture inside spells abject poverty. But simplicity and poverty are not the same thing. As Africans live mostly outdoors, and Europeans live the greater part of their lives indoors, their concepts of accommodation and amenity are different. This outdoor/indoor divide is also one reason why northern hemisphere pundits slip so easily into clichés about overpopulation in African countries. People who live outdoors are more visible than those who stay indoors warming their bottoms on the radiators. The fact that an average African village seems crowded, whereas an average northern European village seems deserted, does not say anything reliable about comparative densities of population.

Quilligan's first impression of the interior of the mud house was of delicious coolness and soft restful light. Because of the absence of unnecessary furniture, there was plenty of space for people, who seemed perfectly comfortable sitting on the floor or on window ledges. Chairs appeared from nowhere for the inspector and for the two "Reverend Fathers," as they were called, who were soon surrounded by a smiling and welcoming audience: Shad's mother, his two small sisters and a teenage brother, various aunts and uncles from the other houses, and droves of children who slotted themselves in wherever there was a space.

It was obvious to Quilligan that, for most of the smaller children, he and Father Dick were the first white men that they had ever seen—or at least the first that they had had an opportunity to examine at close quarters. They set about their investigations with enthusiasm and unchecked by adults, who obviously approved of hands-on research. So, as the white men conversed, the texture of their skin was gently probed by little hands, the hair on their forearms was stroked and combed in every direction, and Quilligan's blue eyes and Father Dick's green ones were scrutinized with solemn attention. It was the hair on their heads that probably intrigued the children most. They seemed enthralled by its seemingly endless possibilities, as they coaxed it discreetly with nimble fingers into shapes and styles that would have cost a king's ransom in any *maison de haute coiffure*.

Shad's mother, Madame Angelina, made a deep impression on the inspector. She had just come in from collecting wood, which she carried back from the bush on her head, followed in crocodile formation by her two little girls, each balancing a bucket of water with apparently effortless ease. Ben, her last remaining man around the house, brought up the rear with a great basin of water cushioned by a tight coil of cloth on his head. Even in her farming clothes, she was a woman of remarkable presence, tall and slim, striking rather than beautiful, a strong person. Quilligan was to say many times later that, from that very first moment, he had said to himself: So this is where those two boys got it!

Madame Angelina was an educated woman, a primary schoolteacher and an active administrator in her local church. She had shown her independence of spirit by resisting the pressure of traditional society to marry again after her husband's death, and most especially by refusing to become a second wife for the senior uncle, whose first wife had borne him no children and was urging him to take a junior wife.

She had also opposed head-on the attempt by powerful traditional cult figures in her village to have her third son, Ben, treated as an *ogbanje,* that is as a spirit child who does not belong fully to this world, but comes and goes from the spirit world in a series of unpredictable incarnations. Ben was seen as suspiciously otherworldly in his reflective quietness and his lack of assertiveness. The received wisdom was that an *ogbanje* child needed plenty of rough treatment if he was not to cause mischief. Madame Angelina had to chase one priest of traditional religion away with blows of a broom before he would leave her child alone. The priest continued to utter blood-curdling curses against her for years afterward—always from a safe distance—but the curses never did her any harm, and the priest never came back for more of her broom.

By now, at the age of fifteen, he had grown bigger and sturdier, and people were beginning to be aware of his hidden strengths. Some were saying that he would be a doctor, others said a reverend father, a teacher, or a great statesman. His mother, who cherished the boy's calm seriousness, his quiet humor, and his sensitivity to other people, told Quilligan, "He belongs to God. He will be a poet, or a great leader, or perhaps he will join the monks at Ewu or Illah. That is another way to serve people." She also told him that, with Shad dead, if Ben did become a monk, Jude would have to come back home, marry within his clan, and raise children for his family.

Quilligan would have loved to speak to this woman on her own. As it was, he had to do the best he could surrounded by the rather stupid uncles and numerous other people who came and went endlessly throughout his visit. He could see that she was heartbroken by the death of her eldest son, and was absolutely at a loss to understand how such a thing could have happened.

"Shad was a good boy, Inspector, through and through. When his father died, he was the man in this house. He could so easily have become difficult and headstrong. But his only thought was to help me. He never disobeyed me, never once. And after he went to Lagos, and then since he traveled out to Europe, he is sending me money every time, every *kobo* he could spare.

"I am feeling his death too much, and his sisters are feeling it everytime. Shad was their little daddy and their big man. They were always waiting for the day when he would come home again. It is God's will, and we must accept it. But how could this thing happen—to Shad? He never did bad to one person in his entire life."

"Madame Angelina, what can I say to you? I am ashamed for my country. We are trying every way to find out what happened, but I admit, we are puzzled. The truth is that we just do not know who did this terrible thing, and why."

"You are trying, Inspector. Thank you. What of Jude?"

"Jude is fine. He is very sad, of course, but he is fine, and he is running his restaurant very well, with the help of . . ."

"Madame Margot."

"Yes, Margot. She is a splendid woman."

"Thank God that she is with him. Shad was praising her every-time when he wrote me letter."

"Madame Angelina, will you help me? Jude does not trust the police. People tell me that the police in this country are not . . . well, not always very . . ."

At this, several people made a strange clicking sound in their throats which Quilligan took to indicate understanding and agreement with what he, or perhaps with what Jude was saying or thinking. He went on:

"To be honest about it, I think that if Jude would trust us—or, to be truthful, if he would trust *me* more, and share his ideas and his suspicions with me, we might make more progress with our inquiries."

She smiled.

"Jude is like his father, Inspector! I will write him a letter and you will bring it. I will tell him to trust you very well."

Professor Lionel Ogogie was an internationally recognized authority on African traditions, folklore, and customs. Even more to the point, as far as Quilligan was concerned, he had his ear firmly to the ground of Nigerian affairs: Ogogie knew what was going on. Why this was so, nobody could quite say. Though not affiliated with any political party—and never having stood for election or served in any administration, civilian or military—Ogogie seemed to have the entree to them all. He was also a very wealthy man, whose business interests, especially in oil and construction, clearly bespoke the backing and consent of the country's movers and shakers.

The most frequently advanced and plausible explanation for Ogogie's influence was that he was high in the echelons of the Ogboni secret society.

Small and bespectacled, a mild, bookish-looking man, with a solemn good-egg bald dome, Lionel Ogogie received Quilligan and Father Dick graciously in his unpretentious office at Ekpoma University, two days after their visit to Shad's family. Father Dick had prepared the ground well. The professor was fully apprised of the inspector's business and immediately took control of the discussion.

"Inspector, Ogboni honor the Yoruba god, Onile. The trouble is that there are four hundred and one Yoruba gods—at the very least—and there are at least four hundred and two different versions of who or what Ogboni might be. You have all sorts of groups and splinter groups who enjoy calling themselves Ogboni. Nobody, but nobody, can give you an authoritative answer about the thoughts and activities of all these different groups."

"But isn't there a serious, or a central, or, let's say, a traditional Ogboni society?"

The professor smiled whimsically, as if considering how much he could tease the inspector without being naughty, then sat up straight and gave a dry cough, like somebody making up his mind to act responsibly.

"Yes, there is. At Father Dick's request, I have made serious inquiries on your behalf in relation to this poor boy, Shadrack Nwachukwu: that is his name?"

"Correct."

"That name means nothing to what you call the 'serious' or 'traditional' Ogboni society. These people are not in the habit of going around torturing or killing anybody, and they had no hand, act, or part in this boy's death. You may take that as definitive."

"As an African, Professor, and as an expert, have you any suggestion to make to me about why a young African man might die in this very unusual way?"

"You mean some sort of *African* reason, don't you, Inspector, as if only Africans could be guilty of such an aberration?"

"Europeans have plenty of aberrations too, but I would tend to know about those, whereas here we have one that I do not recognize; I just thought that perhaps you might."

"Fair enough. My first piece of advice to you is to forget Ogboni, Bakassi Boys, OPC, and all these other Nigerian brotherhoods or societies. The thought of any of these people, in any of their ramifications, the thought of *any* of these murdering some tiny shopkeeper in the back streets of Dublin is, frankly, ridiculous."

"So where does that leave us?"

"It leaves you, Inspector, with whatever number of millions of people you have over there, whoever they are and wherever they may come from."

The professor got up and walked over to the window where he stood looking out for some time. Turning to face the inspector again, he plunged both hands into his trouser pockets, and took up a new phase of what he had obviously intended to say.

"Inspector, let us suppose that this thing had happened here in Ekpoma—I mean the severed leg, the eventual death of the victim. Let us even suppose it was the same unfortunate young man, Shadrack, who had been disposed of—I think I would be looking at two possibilities. Perhaps you should look at the same two possibilities in your own country."

"This sounds very interesting, Professor. What are those two possibilities?"

"The first possibility is student cults. This is a university town. Here, as on many campuses around the country, we have had trouble with these student cults. Most of the time, it is little more than youthful pranks, annoying, disruptive perhaps, usually not very wicked. But on occasion the mischief has tipped over the top, into initiation rites or forms of hazing which go beyond a joke, involving, for instance, ordeals that are sadistic, sexually degrading, or even physically dangerous. Some of these escapades, I regret to say, have proved fatal. I presume you have students in Dublin, Inspector."

"We have, of course, thousands of them. But Shad had nothing to do with the student world."

"So he was hardly a member of a student cult, I agree. That does not mean that he was safe from them."

"Why not?"

"Because students are no respecters of boundaries, and they will try anything. There is an American lady who has written a book recently about a group of Greek students in an American university—I mean students of Greek language and culture— who decide to have a go at an old-time bacchanalia. They get blind drunk, then proceed to rampage around the countryside draped in sheets. In the course of their festivities they come upon an inoffensive farmer going about his legitimate business. They fall upon him, kill him, and probably offer him in sacrifice to one of their Greek gods, as well. It is a novel, Inspector, but such things can happen."

"I could not imagine that happening at Belfield—that is the biggest Dublin campus: still less in Trinity College—they are all Protestants there, for God's sake!"

"Please yourself, Inspector. But I have worked with students all my adult life. The great majority are, as you imply, nice kids.

Even so, I would check them out, if I were you. My experience is that if there is something that really does not make sense, try the students: they probably had a hand in it!"

"Well, what is your second possibility—that you would try here in Ekpoma?"

"Even less applicable, you might think, in your context; but still possible, I assure you. A ritual killing, or perhaps the cutting out or the cutting off of a body part for a ritual purpose. This could be as harmless as taking a mesh of hair or some clippings of fingernails, but it can also target a vital internal organ, a kidney, the liver, the heart. In such cases, the death of the victim is not directly intended, but it is nonetheless inevitable."

"Why in the name of God would somebody do such a thing?"

"Perhaps exactly as you say, 'in the name of God.' As you will know from your Bible, the people of the Old Testament, like all ancient peoples, believed that different animals had to be sacrificed to God, and carefully designated parts of those animals had to be consumed by fire. So there is a religious dimension to it. There is also a magico-medical aspect. The blood of various animals or specific organs were believed to have special powers against specific diseases or against unfriendly spirits, or as a shield against curses. Believe me, Inspector, these ideas are not confined to primitive African savages who know no better. Think of Tobias and his fish!"

"I'm sorry, Professor, I am not with you."

The professor looked amused.

"Dear me, Inspector, don't you know your Bible—and you a Christian, I presume? What about Reverend Father?"

Father Dick shifted uncomfortably. The professor continued:

"Young Tobias went down to the river Tigris to wash his feet. A great fish leapt out of the water. Can you remember what the great fish tried to do?"

The two Christians looked at each other, embarrassed.

"No? My word! Well, I am what you people would call a 'pagan,' but I'll tell you. According to your Holy Bible, the big fish tried *to swallow the boy's foot.* Isn't that interesting, in the context of your present case—or is it just a coincidence?"

Quilligan stared at the professor, astonished.

"You mean . . ."

"No, I don't, Inspector, actually. That bit *is* a coincidence. But let's look at the rest. Tobias and his companion ate some of the fish, salted the rest of it—to eat later on in their journey, but they also kept some of it for other purposes."

Father Dick jumped in hastily, eager to recapture some shred of reputation.

"Ah yes, of course! Tobias cut out the fish's liver, and he used it to cure his father's blindness."

"Reverend Father, I hate to tell you this, especially in the presence of a mere layperson, but that answer would earn you about sixteen percent in a Scripture examination. Tobias cut out the fish's liver, heart, and gall. And he used the gall, not the liver, to cure his father's blindness. Can you remember now what he used the heart and the liver for?"

The priest and the mere layperson looked at each other sheepishly, while the pagan came again to their aid and discomfort.

"You will, I hope, remember that Tobias married the charming but unfortunate Sarah, whose seven previous husbands had each died on the occasion of his first connubial encounter with the young lady, through the intervention of a malicious demon. Tobias, however, had been well primed by his traveling companion,

Azarias—who conveniently happened to be the archangel Raphael in disguise. So, taking the fish's heart and liver, he put them to roast on some burning charcoal serendipitously to hand. The smell of this barbecue so distressed the demon that he fled to Egypt—where, we are told, Raphael, just to be sure, pursued him, clapped him in chains, and strangled him."

"Amazing!" Quilligan exclaimed. "Is that story really in the Bible?"

"It is," Father Dick conceded ruefully.

"Well, my purpose was not to lecture you on biblical exegesis, but to show how the worlds of religion, medicine, demonology, human relations, including romance and sexuality, have all been ritualized around the mysterious properties of various bodily organs—of a fish, in this case, but in other cultures, it could be an animal, or even a human being."

"Yes, but that is all primitive stuff; we don't have that sort of thing nowadays."

"No, Inspector, you think not? Well, in Africa, we certainly do. Your admirable Western press was telling you as recently as last year that thirty or more 'witch doctors,' as they called them, had been arrested in Anambra State for trading in body parts."

"For transplants, was it? That is happening in many countries."

"Not for transplants: for traditional medicine. And in South Africa, the Muti murders are notorious."

"What are they?"

"Inspector, if I may say so, you are exceptionally uninformed. The Muti are probably the world's most dedicated hunters of body parts. They use them for native healing. They do not murder people just for an arm or a leg. That would be wasteful. They murder, then vandalize, taking brain, liver, kidneys, heart, genitals, the lot. Look them up on your www when you get home. I hope you have a strong stomach: you will find photographs there, not easy to look at!"

"Do you think that the Muti could be active in Europe?"

"In the U.K., yes. They are strongly suspected in connection with the death of a boy whose torso was found floating in the Thames a few years ago.

"I think you can forget about the Muti in your own case—if only because it would not be like them to take only one organ, least of all a foot. But, you know, Europe has its own skeletons in the cupboard, if you will pardon the unfortunate expression, its own fetishes, even its own cannibalism. Oh yes, it lifts its ugly head from time to time. Think, too, of the whole vampire thing, the 'living dead' kept alive by human blood—as so excellently described by your own Irish Bram Stoker in *Dracula*.

"Let me tell you something, Inspector. In connection with my work I monitor these things. I am seeing growing evidence in recent years of dark and dangerous ritual practices in various parts of Europe. At least some of these cases involve the mutilation and death of human persons. Do you believe in the devil, Inspector?"

Quilligan was startled.

"I don't quite know . . ."

The professor smiled.

"Well, if there is a devil, there is no reason why he should have to be black, is there—or, still less, African?"

"Of course not. Indeed, Father Dick was just saying the same thing to me a few nights ago."

"Very wise of him, if I may say so. Inspector, you came to Africa to discover what strange African superstitions might have led to the death of this poor boy. I would advise you now to go back home with a different question, indeed two questions:

"Firstly, have your student types been up to something? Especially now when, throughout the developed world, students seem to have lost interest in peace and justice, and social protest—they must be getting pretty bored. They can't study all the time, or drink beer, or pursue their love affairs, can they? Bored students are dangerous. Who knows what they will do?

"The second question is about this ritual killing thing. When religion dies in any civilization or culture, there is a big gap to be filled. Bread and circuses are not enough to fill it all the time. Even football matches are not enough! So what do people turn to instead? You know the saying, The devil makes work for idle hands. Think about that, Inspector—and forget about Africa."

The professor showed his guests out, very politely.

CHAPTER ELEVEN

DURING THE SIX MONTHS THAT JUDE HAD SPENT IN LA-
gos before coming to Ireland he had learned to ride a motorbike. He had even worked for some weeks as an Okada driver,
that is, as a motorbike taximan. Okada is the name of a Nigerian
domestic airline, which some seer or humorist had attached to
those fleets of motorbikes carrying paying passengers that had
suddenly proliferated in Nigerian cities from the early 1990s.
The name had stuck and had spread throughout the entire country as rapidly as the machines themselves.

It was not his own motorbike, of course: he was driving for a
"thick madam" who had six machines droning like hornets
around the Ikeja, Surulere, Maryland, Yaba, and Oshodi districts
of the city. Because Jude was good-looking and good-living, and
honest into the bargain, handing over *all* of what he earned each
day—an unheard-of practice among her drivers—Madame
Oladele was sweet on him, treated him generously, and paid him
well. It was she who eventually bridged the substantial gap between what he had been able to save and what he needed for his
airfare to Ireland, a doubly noble gesture on her part, as she
hated losing him.

To have survived weeks of weaving in and out of Lagos traffic without so much as a scratch to his passengers, his machine, or himself was eloquent testimony to Jude's mastery of the Lagos rodeo—one of world's most challenging circuits. His achievement was all the greater for the fact that he regularly had anything between one and four passengers lined up on the pillion seat behind him. In Africa, unlike Europe, irrespective of gender assortment, such extreme physical proximity, indeed promiscuity, occasions neither embarrassment nor lubricity.

On the basis of this experience, Jude's helpful neighbor in Dublin, Tunde, was quite willing to lend him his own machine. The Yoruba presumed that he needed wheels by night to progress some nascent love affair. He was happy to support any initiative that might cheer the boy up and get him going again after his recent tragedy.

It was nearly eleven o'clock when Jude kicked the starter outside the darkened restaurant and headed into the night. He took Bolton Street, into Church Street, and across the river, where he quickly ran into problems with one-way traffic systems. At such a late hour there were not too many cars about, so he had scope for trial and error and was soon past the final booby trap at Upper Leeson Street and bombing out toward Donnybrook, Mount Merrion, Stillorgan, and Foxrock. It was easier than he had expected. He just followed the route he had taken weeks before in the bus: due south on the dual roadway until he saw Foxrock church at the bottom of the hill.

Having turned off the motorway, he cruised along Westminster Road on gentle throttle, cutting the engine fifty or sixty yards back from the Finnerty residence and freewheeling the rest of the way down. His momentum carried him through the gates and halfway up the avenue. The house was in darkness and there were no cars parked anywhere in sight. Jude wheeled his machine into a copse of small trees just off the tarmac and continued light-footed toward the house. The burglar alarm system was prominently signaled by a belligerently red box high on the gable corner. He risked a few glances through lower story windows, being careful not to so much as touch the window glass. He noted dust covers on furniture in the sitting room where Mrs. Finnerty had received him briefly on his first visit. He was not very interested in the main house. He had hardly been in there, and he doubted if Shad had spent much time in those formal rooms, either. It was the studio he had come to revisit. There, he felt, was where the spirits were calling him.

Going around by the side of the house, Jude noted that the elaborate dog and cat feeding area, with its personalized crockery for Tiger, Buttons, and Marmalade, which had so intrigued him on his previous visit as typical European lunacy, was no longer there on its terrace. All the signs seemed to say that Mrs. Finnerty had indeed gone away and that the house was unoccupied. This was what he needed, to get into that studio, to sit there in the dark without fear of interruption, to pray, to talk to Shad, who had spent long hours there, half-naked and defenseless against what they were planning to do to him. Jude would listen to his brother's spirit, to the spirits of his ancestors. He was being summoned here, he knew it, drawn like iron to a magnet. He would enter, he would listen and see. Then he would know what to do. By God's grace, he would do it.

With Providence as his tailwind, Jude was not surprised to find the studio unprotected by burglar alarms. He could effect an entry through an imperfectly closed window in the rear without breaking or forcing anything. He stood there, his arms stretched above his head, his hands already braced against the window frame to lift himself up to where he could kneel on the narrow sill. Momentarily, he let his forehead rest against the cool glass of the window. He knew that he would not come out from this night's experience unscathed. He felt driven to know the truth, but he would probably have to pay a price for that knowledge. He prayed that it would not destroy him.

Landing lightly in the kitchenette from the window, Jude got from there into a short corridor. He had had the presence of mind to bring a flashlight, with which he was able to explore this back section of the studio rapidly without turning on any lights. Next to the kitchenette, where he noted that the fridge had been cleared out and left open, there was a small bathroom and toilet, then a broom cupboard, and, beside the entrance to the studio itself, a storeroom lined with shelves well stocked with art materials of every sort, together with several small pieces of half-finished pottery and sculpture.

His memory of the studio, he found, was quite accurate, and very little seemed changed since his last visit. It was tidier and less cluttered. There had certainly been an attempt at rationalization and some serious discarding of excess paraphernalia, the sort of clearing out one does before going away on a long journey. There were good blinds fitted to the windows in this room, but he was afraid to turn on a light because of the ample skylights. Even if the house were unoccupied, as he now believed it was, he could not take the risk of a light being seen through the trees from a neighboring residence where the occupants, knowing that Mrs. Finnerty was away, might call the police. Besides, the night was not dark. He could manage quite well, at least until he found something worth closer examination.

Jude sifted and rummaged desultorily for perhaps half an hour, without finding anything to engage his interest. There was nothing he could identify in any medium as a drawing or a portrayal of Shad. Eventually, he was down to a four-drawer filing cabinet and a large, built-in cupboard, both of them locked. Perhaps one of these contained some vital clue. Should he break them open? He had never done anything like that in his life and he was not at all comfortable with the idea. It was one thing to slip in the window of somebody's studio, for a very good reason. To vandalize their furniture and pry into secrets that might not concern him at all: these were very different matters. He would not do it—unless the spirits . . . in which case, they would need to make their orders very clear!

He sat down on a camp chair, the same chair—he noted after he had done it—that he had occupied on his last visit to this room. He remained there for a long time, eyes closed, head bowed, his hands limp on his knees. He prayed a little. Mostly he just waited. Perhaps he dozed, his heart still vigilant.

His eyes were open again. A shaft of moonlight was playing on the bookcases against the wall facing him across the room. He was not alone, he knew it, and he did not have to wonder what he would do next. He stood up and walked straight to the bookcases.

There they were, the five large, white volumes produced by Harvard University. He remembered that name distinctly. Harvard is one of many names for the utterly unattainable, an inaccessible place that people like Jude know about as somewhere not to even dream of when they lie awake at night, unable to sleep, hungry, imagining impossible things for a golden future that will never be.

He remembered the title, too, *The Image of the Black in West-*

ern Art. He had thought about that title a lot since he had last been here. What it meant was: how white people have depicted black people down through the ages, how they have *seen* them, and therefore how they have thought about them. He remembered the pain and the anger he had felt the last time he had taken one of these volumes in his hands: Wilson and the body-parts artists who used yet annihilated blackness, and the grosser, yet less dishonest forms of slavery and exploitation, with the rags and the nakedness, the coffin ships, the dogs, the whips, and the chains.

This time he felt calmer and stronger. Still, he avoided the right side of the stack, from which the volume that had upset him so much had come. Instead he pulled out the first volume in the series from the left and carried it over to Mrs. Finnerty's desk. He turned on the table lamp, which, he was happy to discover, had a wide shade, throwing light downward onto the desk in a wide pool, while preventing any telltale beams rising toward the skylights in the ceiling.

Volume one, on its cover, professed to deal with the period "from the Pharaohs to the Fall of the Roman Empire." Jude was enthralled by everything he saw in this volume: frescoes and statues, figures in stone, wood, bronze, and terracotta, jugs and vessels in the shape of human heads, mosaics depicting landscapes, and hunting scenes with black huntsmen and all kinds of fabulous animals. The huntsmen, he noticed, were not always winning: there were several pictures showing a lion or a crocodile making a good meal of an unsuccessful adversary. Equal opportunity was more respected in this volume than in the one he had seen last time he was here. There were no slaves or ex officio losers, neither people nor animals.

He loved the unmistakably African *feel* to many of the pieces in this book, so much so that he doubted if any white man could possibly have made them. On the other hand, he was also very taken by a *not* very African, but nonetheless beautiful, painted wooden box from the tomb of Tutankhamen. Here he saw the boy pharaoh in his chariot waging war against black warriors who, if clearly getting the worst of the engagement, were dying with great elegance. To level the balance once again, he was fascinated to read in one of the learned articles presenting these images that several of the pharaohs had themselves been Ethiopian, and therefore, as black as himself.

Jude particularly loved the shining black glazes on some of the pottery pieces. They captured perfectly the shimmering, sensuous luminosity of black skin. Indeed, in whatever art form they were depicted, the warriors, athletes, and musicians all looked magnificent, while some of the female figures were bewitchingly beautiful beyond his wildest dreams. So vivid in his reactions to visual art, of which he had seen too little, Jude gazed openmouthed at these goddess women, desiring them with all the passion of his youthful heart and hormones.

An owl screeched, sudden and shrill, beating wings furiously against the window behind his head. Jude nearly jumped out of his skin with fright. Dramatic sublimation for lustful feelings. When his heart, still thumping painfully, had slithered back down his throat from behind his teeth, he realized at once what the spirits were sternly telling him: *You are here on serious business: Get on with it!*

He ran back guiltily to the bookshelves and stowed away the beguiling volume, reaching hastily for the next one. They were not in strict order on the shelf, so this time he came away with volume two, part two, which he carried rapidly back to his desk.

This volume was one of two ranging "from the Early Christian

Era to the Age of Discovery." On the dust cover, and reproduced fully inside, there was a magnificent painting by Hieronymus Bosch of a tall black man in sumptuous white robes, representing the black king, among the Magi at the Christmas Crib. Towering majestically over every other figure in the painting, the black king held in his hand a precious jar of myrrh, on which perched a live bird, which, according to the learned notes, was a pelican, symbolizing Christ the Savior. Jude was astonished by the extraordinary resemblance between this young king and an Igbo man, called Aloy, whom he had known in Lagos. The likeness was not merely facial, it extended to the smallest details of poise and carriage. Was it possible, he wondered, for people to come back and live again after hundreds of years?

When he had looked at this painting for a long time, he again became guiltily conscious that he was wasting time. On a quick impulse, he turned over fifteen or twenty pages together. And there it was: leaping up at him like a deadly snake, to strike again and again, straight in his face, before he could make the slightest move to shield himself. Eyes wide, mouth gaping, his hands gripping the seat of his chair, he sat there, paralyzed, transfixed. After what seemed an age he became conscious of a distant whimpering sound, a voice sobbing over and over again: *Jesus, O Jesus, Jesus Christ help us, O Jesus, help us, O Jesus.* It was his own voice.

Slowly, and with great difficulty, he forced himself to distance this thing from his eyes, to push it away physically, so that he could at least start to *think* about it. He had to break this spell. He had to *do* something, however simple or purposeless. He stood up and backed away from the desk. He stood at the window. He paced the room, once, twice, three times. He tidied books on a side table. He went out to the bathroom, where he urinated and blew his nose into his hands, and drank water. Then he stood again for a while, hands hanging by his sides, just breathing in and out. He brought water into the studio and poured it onto the potted plants on the windowsill. He went back and fetched more. Then he brushed dust off the windowsill with his sleeve. Then he just stood again.

One final deep breath. Then he turned abruptly and strode back to the desk. Searching, he found an A4 writing pad in one drawer and a Biro in another. He sat down and forced himself to look again, and to write.

I am seeing this picture in this book. It is having a whole page in this book. Near me, in the front of this picture in this book, a black boy is lying on his back. He is lying on the ground. He is propping himself up on his left elbow. His left leg have been cut off at his knee. He is holding the stump of his cut-off leg with his right hand. He is having dreadful pain. He is making an agony face. He is crying and crying and crying too much, because thay have took away his leg and he can no walk again, and he is hurting too bad. And he is dying. This boy is Shad.

He stopped and wiped his eyes and nose with his sleeve. Then he grabbed up his Biro again and stabbed violently at his left hand with the point of the pen, to cause pain, to beat himself like a poor jaded animal, to force himself to continue.

This is an olden days picture. Behind this boy, and also going like him right across the picture from one side to the other side, there is a rich white man lying on a bed. It is a rich white man's bed. His head is seatting nicely on two fat pillows. The black boy have no pillows. The white man is having very costly covers on his bed—every this-thing for him is standard. The black boy have no covers and no bed and he have no leg again and he is crying, crying very plenty.

There are two white men standing at the bed. They are wearing very fine olden days clothes. They are doctors and dressed very decent with big hat on their heads. One of this doctors is feeling the white man's poulse in his wrist and he is looking at a medicine something in his other hand. The other doctor is standing at the end of the bed. He is fixing the black boy's cut-off leg onto the white man's cut-off leg stump.

This is written beside this picture in this book: "Miracle of the Black Leg, Valladolid, Spain, mid-XVI century." This is also written, "One step further and we have the Valladolid relief. The holy physicians, intent on their work, are completely indifferent to the black man whose face is contorted with pain as he holds the stump of his leg in his right hand."

THE HOLY PHYSICIANS! EAT SHIT! EAT SHIT, YOU FUCKERS!

Jude turned off the desk lamp and sat for a long time in the dark, his face in his hands. He felt very tired and hungry, and deeply sad. He had sometimes felt sad before in his life, like when Shad died he had felt very sad. But now, for the first time ever in his life, he thought, he knew what "depression" meant. Was this really all that Shad's life was worth? Then was anybody's life worth anything? Was his own life worth anything? Did it mean anything?

At last, he forced himself to turn on the light again, to read more, and to write more notes. He no longer had the energy to watch his English. He just had to write down facts, without thinking how to say them, or even what he thought of them. There would be time for that tomorrow and for many days to come.

There are four more pictures in this book about this story of the Black Man's cut-off leg. In all this four other pictures, the black man is dead. Sometimes, as well as they have cut off and take his leg, they have also give him back the white man's cut-off leg, like tit for tat!

The book say that this story come from a book called, "The Golden Legend" which was wrote by a man called Jacob of Voragine thousands years ago. This story is about St. Cosmas and St. Damian, that is the two doctors. The story tells that the two saints which is doctors too go cure one sick white man with bad leg, by cut off his bad leg and take his good leg from one healthy black man who is dead and bury, and stick it on the white man—who get up quick and run around very fast and easy.

When he had finished writing, Jude pushed his chair back violently from the table, filled his lungs with air to bursting, then emptied them out in one long, hoarse, gasping cry of anger and disgust. Then, as if he had vomited out demons, he stood up quietly, collected his pages, folded them, and put them in his pocket. He replaced the art book on its shelf, tidied away the writing pad and Biro, turned off the light, and left through the studio door, pulling it closed behind him.

Heading back toward the city, cool air rushing in his face as he accelerated, Jude felt refreshed and strangely at peace. He had done what he had to do. Once more he had listened and obeyed, and he had suffered for it. Now he would eat something and sleep. This time, he knew, his sleep would be undisturbed. What he had learned was horrible beyond belief, but he knew now what he had to do, and with God's help, he would do it.

———

Jim Quilligan and Molly Power arrived at the restaurant before eleven o'clock the next morning. Quilligan had arrived back in Ireland early the previous afternoon and had slept most of the time since then. Now he was eager to share his experiences and to implement all sorts of good intentions concerning Jude and any other Nigerians who might cross his path.

Jude had slept well. He felt calm but tired, and ravenously hungry, as he had not eaten since noon on the previous day, and had been too exhausted to eat when he got back at four o'clock in the morning. Margot, who seemed to know his physical and psychological needs without asking, had served him up an enormous hot breakfast of yam slices and beans. He ate it all and felt better. Now, to his surprise, he was actually enjoying the police visit.

Molly, Jude already liked and trusted. Quilligan's unfeigned delight in everything he had heard and seen in Nigeria amused and pleased him. He was very happy to hear news of his mother and family and to receive their letters. Quilligan had put his films into a one-hour service near his home the previous day and was, therefore, able to hand over several nice pictures he had made at Nnewi. He had also brought Jude a big jar of his mother's *miemie*, which brought tears of pleasure to the boy's eyes.

The visit went well from everybody's point of view. They did not talk about the murder investigation until the very end. When Molly said that she had to be going, Quilligan told her to take the car, adding that perhaps Jude would walk him some bit of the way back to Store Street. Jude guessed that this bit had been prearranged, but he recognized that it was well-intentioned and he went out willingly with the inspector. They did not go toward Store Street, but strolled up to Parnell Square where they sat on a bench.

"Jude, as I told you, I went to Nigeria for a meeting about

crimes against children. But Shad's case was never far from my mind. I talked to many wise people who advised me about—let's say, African ways of thinking and doing things. But the most helpful conversation I had was with your mother. I am sure she will tell you some of that herself in her letter. She is a very lovely woman, and very strong."

"I thank Jesus that she is strong. I feared that she might be beaten down by Shad's death."

"She is very sad, of course, but she has great faith. She trusts God."

He paused, then took his courage in both hands.

"Jude, your mother also trusts me, and she wants you to trust me. She will tell you that in her letter. I am not God, Jude, I don't have to tell you that, but you and I both want the same thing. We want to catch Shad's killer. And to do that, we must help each other. Two heads are better than one."

"Inspector, if this murderer is caught, what will happen to him?"

"If he is convicted of murder, he will get life imprisonment."

"Will he not be put to death?"

"No, we have no capital punishment in this country."

"Somebody told me that life imprisonment means seven or eight years."

"Sometimes, depending on circumstances, people can get out earlier."

"'Depending on circumstances,' does that mean that some murders are not very serious?"

"All murders are serious, very serious, but . . ."

His voice trailed away. Was he losing the boy again? Jude cut in on his thoughts. He held out his hand.

"Inspector, I am sorry that I did not trust you. Where I come from the police is not always very honest. I see now, you are a good man—as Miss Molly is a nice woman."

That had to be progress, Quilligan thought. He took the offered hand and shook it. Jude continued.

"Perhaps it is the law I do not trust to punish murder as my fathers wish it to be punished. People is telling me that if this murderer is caught, he may not even be found guilty of murder: the white men will let him out on some small, small excuse, now or after a few years."

"Jude, my job is to catch murderers. The prosecution service puts them before the court. The jury finds them innocent or guilty. The judge imposes sentence. A court of appeal may vary that finding or that sentence. And even after all that, prison authorities, or the minister for justice, or some other authority, may shorten or change the sentence in some way. I can only do my own job. I promise you that, for Shad's sake, for your mother's sake, for your own sake, and because I want to be happy in my own heart, I will do my job in this case to the very best of my ability. I cannot answer for all those other people—but I am sure that they are all honorable people who will also do their jobs according to their conscience."

Jude took his hand and shook it again.

"I believe you, Inspector, and I am grateful. My ancestors will bless you."

"Really?" said Quilligan, trying not to sound amused.

"Yes, they will; but I don't think they will be pleased with all these other people. You know the wise saying about the bad kitchen."

"No. What saying?"

"Too many cooks is pissing in the soup!"

Quilligan laughed.

"We don't say it quite like that."

"Well, we call it 'pissing in the soup.' In my country, if the police is sure they have the murderer, they often shoot him on the side of the road. Of course, they say he tried to run away, just for make happy the judges who think they are the only important people."

"Jude, tell me straight. Do you know things about Shad's murder that you have not told me?"

Jude tilted his head sideways and thought for a while before he spoke.

"Yes, Inspector, I will not talk lie, I think I know things that you do not know. Give me small time, I beg. There is some small thing I must do. Then I will talk to you."

"Promise that you are not going to harm somebody—or execute him, on orders from your ancestors!"

Jude smiled and did not reply.

After the sad debacle at his lookout post in Temple Bar, Pita stayed away from there for several days. Soon, however, not seeing what else he could do to help Jude catch the murderer, he gritted his teeth and faced back to the scene of that bitter disappointment, ready to take up his day-long vigils once again. Turning the corner into the frontline street, he was already tensing muscles to spring up the side of the Dumpster, when a good-humored Dublin voice hailed him:

"Hey, Blessed Martin, where do you think you are going?"

The manner of address did not surprise him. It was not the first time he had been called "Blessed Martin." The Dublin poor had a great devotion, going back over many years, to the black Peruvian Dominican saint, Martin de Porres. Even after the pope had promoted Martin to being fully paid-up Saint Martin, Dubliners still called him what they had always called him, Blessed Martin, or even, Saint Blessed Martin.

When black boys first began to appear in the streets of Dublin, they were regularly addressed, with wry affection, as Blessed Martin, especially as the boxes used to collect pennies from the poor for the foreign missions used to have a little black boy made of plaster kneeling on top, who was wired to nod appreciatively each time a coin fell through the slot. Those humble boxes "for the black babies" probably did more than anything else to prepare a reasonably enlightened reception for real-life black people when eventually they began to be seen around the city.

There was also a no doubt well-intentioned, but incredibly ill-conceived, luxury model of the black baby boxes. This box had the usual little black boy kneeling beside the money slot, ready to acknowledge subscriptions with grateful nods. But his gratitude did not stop there. The more money that went in, the less black in the face he became, until eventually, at around fifteen shillings and nine pence, his face had become shining white. A truly amazing combination of ingenious technology and ingenuous theology, and innocently racist to an appalling degree.

When the first prominent black football player was signed by a Dublin soccer club, the city took him to its heart as its very own black baby. Splendid in defense as in attack, he was above all a magnificent striker. The only problem was that the "baby" had a name about fourteen syllables long and included unpronounceable combinations of x, y, and z. So each time that his team moved in for the kill at Dalymount or Tolka Park, the cry went up from the bleachers, in the unmistakable cadences of Old Dublin:

Give it to Blessed Martin!!

For Pita, then, it was a friendly greeting, but it marked the end of this road. In the interval of his absence, the builder had come back and was now firmly in possession of the site and of his lookout post. Pita grinned foolishly, waved, and was gone. An orderly retreat, this time, but he had been beaten back yet again. What next? he wondered. A second front: but where? How?

It was the evening of Quilligan's visit. The meal was over. A few stragglers remained in the restaurant. Pita was sitting at a table in the corner working on some project for Peggy Breen. Jude came out of the kitchen and went over to sit at his table.

"Colonel Pita, are you ready for a dangerous mission, deep into enemy territory?"

Pita laughed, pleased and flattered.

"*Yessah!* Big Chief General! Now?"

"No, tomorrow. Can you be here by seven o'clock in the morning?"

"Let me sleep here tonight, then I'll surely be here tomorrow. Where are we going?"

"I cannot tell you that tonight—for a reason that you will understand, and agree with, later."

"Can I bring my bow and arrow? Uchedike have make me a very good ones."

"No. We are not expecting crocodiles. Besides, this is an undercover mission."

"'Undercover'? What is undercover?"

"Secret. It is spy work. We must not be noticed."

"Aha! I will make myself small."

Jude carefully omitted to say that this would not be difficult.

Superintendent Denis Lennon, Sergeant Molly Power, and their respective spouses, Mary, and Jan-Hein, the Dutch art expert, were having dinner with Jim and Ann Quilligan and their three teenage children. This was to celebrate the itinerant's return from Africa and to hear his inevitable repertoire of hair-raising stories. Even if most of these would require a twenty percent discount for imagination and value-added taxidermy, they were sure to be thrilling and highly entertaining.

Quilligan was at the top of his form. He started before the meal, as was only right, with a heart-searing account of the Benin conference on children, about which he had already spoken at length with Sheila Hegarty on the telephone. Later, as the meal produced its convivial effects, impressions, impersonations, and anecdotes flowed prodigally from the intrepid explorer. Ann and their three children had already heard dozens of these "Jungle Jim Quilligan" stories in the twenty-four hours since his arrival. They noted with amusement, and without surprise, that most of the stories, like good yogurt cultures, had fermented mysteriously overnight, propagating themselves to several sizes larger than life. For instance, yesterday's brief encounter with the soldier ants had become by this evening a tropical saga of life-and-death proportions.

Soldier ants are certainly worthy of respect. Not even the most venemous snake in the jungle takes them lightly. If you fall and break your leg in the bush or are, by reason of inebriation or for any other reason, unable to move, enough of the soldier ants could lick your bones clean in the space of one night. That is, if they settled down to eat you, there and then, as fast food. Their normal procedure is rather different. They arrive, cheek by jowl and bumper to bumper, in great columns, dozens deep and tens of thousands long. Their first task is to throw several cordons around the target victim or area, so that, even if their quarry fights its way through two or three lines of assailants, there will always be more waiting in the strategic reserve to bring it down.

Then the specialist ants go to work: some stabbing the victim into submission, others carving it into manageable joints, others transporting these joints away for storage in their home-sweet-home anthill—which may be a hundred yards away or more. Yet others lie in wait for blunderers like Quilligan who stick their big hooves into the middle of the party. There are also engineer ants, who form bridges with their bodies, so that meat can be brought over window frames or down steep steps, or they can even make rafts of themselves so that it can be carried away across water.

Quilligan had left Father Dick after their prolonged evening chat, pleasantly refreshed with beer and conversation. He had to walk across the open compound to the bijou pavilion where he was lodged. Passing in front of the kitchen, which also opened into the compound, he was vaguely conscious of having walked through something—leaves perhaps. Nothing happened until he had gone on several paces and was mounting the three steps to his pavilion. At that exact moment, he was smitten with acute agony between the toes of each foot in their open sandals, behind his left knee, and on the most tender surface of his right testicle. Almost immediately, the other knee, the remaining toes, and the outstanding testicle were annexed and enfolded in one and the same excruciating anguish.

Plunging a frantic hand to the most accessible of his torments, he felt his finger promptly skewered by what he saw to be—upon lifting the trembling digit to his wincing face—a gigantic ant with pincers that any dentist would die for. The only possible solution was to throw modesty to the wind, tearing off all his clothes, then to rake ten fingers wildly in every direction, plucking desperately at all the little places where these ruthless paratroopers had landed and were already hard at work, carving him up into handy joints ready for transportation to the anthill.

When Dick Dorr, who had been watching from the house, had managed to control his laughter, he explained that the soldier ants arrive once or twice a year, unannounced, to clear the cockroaches out of his kitchen. You could fight them with paraffin or water. The only result of that would be to make them break formation and resort to guerilla tactics—at which they are even more dangerous. The best thing was to give them vacant possession of the kitchen, which they would then leave as they had come, in good military formation, as soon as the morning sun began to grow hot.

Besides, the ants do a remarkably thorough job. African cockroaches are an inch long. One year Father Dick had calculated the number of them taken out, by the simple expedient of counting how many wings were left behind after carving. The impressive result was that, in the space of one night, one hundred and eighty cockroaches had been dislodged from behind cookers and under presses in his kitchen. That had to be good for hygiene, one would think.

After dinner, they talked a bit about Shad's case. Molly told Quilligan about the letter she had received through Lennon suggesting that there had been a previous case of amputation, also of a leg, and perhaps even an attempted regrafting. Here Jan-Hein, the art specialist, who normally stayed out of police matters, threw in what he called a curious parallel.

"An occasional theme in northern Italian painting, around

about 1370, was a story from the *Legenda Aurea* about the two saintly doctors, Cosmas and Damian, who cured a man's diseased leg by replacing it with a leg from a black man who had just died."

"Isn't that fascinating!" exclaimed Mary Lennon. "Do you mean to say that they had the concept of organ transplants, what, seven hundred years ago?"

"Well, it was a miracle, of course, but there is nonetheless a strictly medical side to it. The actual story is much older than the Golden Legend. It goes right back to the Greek life of the saints. The Greeks were much more scientific and less superstitious than the medievals."

Lennon sat forward, interested:

"Well and good, Jan-Hein, but surely it is all pure pious nonsense in any language. Where do you see any science in such a fable?"

"Look at the story closely, Denis. You have here a white man, who is the patient, and a black man, who supplies the remedy. In the Greek version, at least, that probably has nothing to do with racism or exploitation. It is simply an application of one of the fundamental principles of Greek medicine, as laid down by the great Hippocrates, and taken up by Galen, and indeed by all of the ancient medicine."

"What principle?"

"The principle of *contraria contrariis*, meaning that you cure a sickness by using an *opposite* remedy. You cure hot with cold, moist with dry, acid with alkali, sour with sweet, so on. And in this case, you cure white with black. So you see, that is what the story means: a miracle, certainly, but a miracle that follows best practice."

"That's neat!" Molly exclaimed.

"It may be neat," Lennon replied, "but it would certainly be re-assuring, if we had a few paintings of white chaps donating their leg ends to patch up some black men—just to level the pitch."

Jan-Hein shook his head.

"That we do not have, I'm afraid. I should say that the reason I know a bit about all this is that the theme of the black leg had a late flowering in Antwerp with a Dutch artist, Ambrosius Francken, whom I have been studying recently. He inherits the later Spanish tradition which, I am sorry to say, took a pretty insensitive, indeed a brutal attitude to blacks and to native Indians. In some of those later pictures, around about the 1590s, the black guy isn't even dead when they come to collect his leg—without anesthetic, of course."

"Jesus!" exclaimed Quilligan.

"Yes. It is the age of the *conquistadores,* don't forget. Those were tough people, with unsentimental attitudes toward native populations. As far as they were concerned, the natives were there to be used. End of story!"

"I would not tell all this to Mr. Jude, if I were you," Lennon advised.

"Good God, no!" Quilligan agreed. "He is very sensitive. It would upset him seriously. Besides, he wouldn't have a bull's notion what you were talking about."

"I suppose not."

"I wouldn't be so sure," Molly said.

"No? Well, anyhow, this is all interesting, but it has nothing to do with anything. Okay?"

The question was rhetorical. Nobody answered, and they went on to look at Jim's photographs.

"Just look at this one."

"Oh my God, it's a snake!" exclaimed Molly. "Is he dangerous?"

"Deadly! He is the black snake, a cobra—not the spitting one: the other guy."

"What is he doing?" Molly asked.

"He is trying to swallow a toad. But the toad has puffed himself up, so the snake can't get him in or out of his mouth. Look, he is coiling himself around the toad, trying to crush him down to size—so that he can swallow him down."

"Weren't you brave to go so near!"

"Yes, I was!"

The children cheered with delight. They loved the honesty with which their dad always told people how marvelous he was.

CHAPTER TWELVE

I T WAS MINUTES TO EIGHT O'CLOCK AS JUDE AND HIS PILLION passenger pulled away from the restaurant curbside on Tunde's motorbike and nosed into the morning traffic. Not quite Lagos at rush hour, Dublin was, if anything, even more frustrating. At least, in Lagos, an Okada driver could be doing something useful. He could, for instance, weave in and out of the stalled traffic much more brazenly than would be thought acceptable in Dublin—why, even the stalled traffic would be weaving in and out of itself! He could run upstream against traffic, coming on the "wrong" side of the road. He could mount the sidewalk and nudge pedestrians out of his way for a few meters at a time, or whiz through the forecourts of filling stations. If he got really lucky, he could even provide an unofficial outrider service for military vehicles, which often had soldiers riding on the running boards, wielding whips, or smashing the side mirrors of trucks with their rifle butts or barrels, if the drivers did not dematerial-ize in time to let the army pass.

Pita held on behind, taking note of the route as they went. Down to the river, up the hill, past a first big church (Christ

Church Cathedral), past a second big church (St. Patrick's Cathedral), then off to the left, over a smaller river (the Grand Canal), and south again. Finally, off the High Street of what must once have been a distinct little town, before Dublin City gobbled it up, and immediately into a quieter suburb. Jude drove along by a thick privet hedge, then turned into a big parking lot in front of what seemed like a small hospital or clinic. There was a formal-looking notice board at the entrance, presumably saying where this was, but Pita found the Gothic script impossible to read at speed, and they were past it and heading for the quietest end of the parking lot before he could begin to try.

Jude stopped, pushed the motorbike into the shrubbery, and gestured Pita to follow him into the cover of some rhododendron bushes. They were perhaps forty yards from the main entrance to the building and had a good view over most of the parking lot.

"Jude, what is this place?"

"It doesn't matter, Pita; I'll tell you later. For now, I just want you to look at everybody who comes in or goes out. If you see somebody who you recognize, tell me at once—quietly."

It did not take the boy long to work it out.

"Aha! You think I will see the man who carry Shad that night, the man I have been hunting for weeks and weeks?"

Jude nodded reluctantly.

"Yes now, but ask me no more questions. I don't want to be . . . I want you to make your very own choice your very self," Jude said.

"I will!"

They waited an hour, two hours. Pita, back in hunter mode, was squatting cross-legged, and apparently weightless, on two slender branches, five feet above the ground, the top of his head cresting like some exotic black flower amidst the purple head-size rhododendron blossoms in green seas of foliage. Patient, intent, eager eyes darting in every direction, ears alert, nostrils flared as if to scent his prey, his mind was not idle either while he waited.

"See all this big black cars is coming, going, coming everytime; and this big black vans for dead person."

"Hearses."

"Horses? They is too many. What is this house? Is it hospital? Bad hospital, where all the sick ones is dying."

"It is a funeral home."

Pita laughed softly. He had never heard of such a thing.

"Jude, you are too funny; you talk joke everytime."

"Suit yourself."

"Mr. Finnerty, I thought you would like to know: there was an attempt at a break-in out here at the house."

"When?"

"I'm not sure. In the last week anyhow. It's on the security camera, the front of the house camera."

"Did the alarm go off?"

"No, it seems not, and the police heard nothing. Perhaps the guy didn't try very hard, but you can see him climbing up on the drawing room windowsill and looking in. He gets down then and walks out of the picture. More like a curious tourist than a robber. One thing is funny, though—I mean funny peculiar."

"Yeah. What's that?"

"He is black."

"Black?"

"The robber, or whatever, he was a black man."

Finnerty lowered the telephone from his head and ran the handset thoughtfully along his chin. His eyes were hard.

"Mr. Finnerty, are you there?"

"Yes, Jack. Sorry, somebody just came in. Did you erase the security film?"

"Oh no, sir. Mrs. Finnerty . . . used to say never to do that, without checking with one of you."

"Good. Are you there today?"

"No sir, I was in yesterday to do the garden. I just checked the camera before I left. I called you when I got home but you had left already."

"Thanks, Jack. It is probably nothing. Still, I'll try to get out there tomorrow or the next day and take a look, just in case."

The undertaker replaced the receiver. Without checking with any of his staff, he walked quickly out of his office, along the thick carpeting of his private corridor, into the plush solemnity of the reception area, and out into the open air. He went straight to his green Bentley in its reserved parking space, and drove away.

Pita did not have to look twice. Already before Finnerty had cleared the funeral home entrance, his small hand was clutching at Jude's sleeve.

"Jude, look now, this is him!"

"Where? Quick, show me, Pita!"

"Look! He come front; he go this side!"

They crouched down instinctively. But Jude had seen, and he knew that the boy was right. This was the man who had been pointed out to him in the cemetery as Patrick Finnerty, the undertaker, the man whose wife used to paint Shad, the same woman who owned those horrible art books about black slaves, and whips, and rags, and dogs, and body parts, and "saintly doctors" cutting the legs off black boys to cure rich, ugly, old white men. And now, as Pita's instant recognition had proved beyond the shadow of a doubt, this was the man who had taken Shad away on the night when he was murdered. Jude was confident that, if there were fingerprints on the cigarette box that had been thrown into Pita's Dumpster, these would confirm the accuracy of the boy's identification.

"Keep down!"

The man drove past, within yards of their hiding place. Pita squeezed Jude's arm again, signaling his growing certainty, the nearer the man came, that this was indeed the person who had taken Shad to his death. When the car had driven off, the boy turned to Jude eagerly.

"That is him, Jude. Is this the one you brought me here to see?"

"Yes, Pita, his very self!"

"How did you know he would be here?"

"He owns this place. He is Mr. Finnerty, the man who paid for Shad's burial."

"Did he kill Shad?"

"He took him away that night. You saw that yourself. Shad's chaplet, that he lost, was found in his funeral car—and there are other things, too, things I found out at his house—or at his wife's house. If he did not kill Shad, he or she is knowing who did."

"What you go do now?"

"Well, I must go work now, but I will be thinking all this things in my heart. Tonight I will write down every big and small thing I know in very fine order. Tomorrow I will give all what I have put down to Inspector Quilligan and Miss Molly."

"Can I come, too?"

Jude smiled at his eagerness.

"What! Do you like the police?"

"No, but I like Miss Molly."

His face darkened, which meant he was blushing.

"*EeEEee!*" Jude exclaimed in the rising-falling intonation which expresses astonishment. "So, you are romancing the policewoman!"

Blushing even more furiously, Pita pushed the motorbike roughly out onto the tarmac.

"Come on now, hurry, Jude! I am very busy."

"*Eheh*, so it seems!" Jude exclaimed, laughing.

Finnerty parked in front of the house. He had not lived here much over the last fifteen years, and not at all since . . . recent events. This time, she had more or less put him out. Still, they had a reasonably civilized working arrangement, especially in relation to property and business matters. This included keeping an eye on her house and car whenever she was away. He did this out of some sort of residual affection, but also out of self-interest: directly or indirectly, he was the one who would have to pay if there was any loss or damage.

He examined the outside of the house cursorily, then let himself in at the hall door. Scarcely bothering to look around inside, he made straight for the study, where the gardener had left the film taken from the principal security camera, which was concealed in a gargoyle at the top of the front porch. This camera worked in sync with a security light, both tripping on when a single sensor was activated. One short sequence had been recorded. He sat down in the study to watch it.

A young African man is standing on the front steps. He approaches the hall door, tries to look through the letter box, which is enclosed on the inside, and through the glass panels to either side of the door—where he cannot have seen much either because the panels are narrow and glazed with opaque stained glass. He then cranes his neck at one or two windows, particularly at the drawing room window, where he climbs onto the sill, balancing there on his knees, and tilts his head at every angle to see as much as he can inside the room. Finnerty found himself admiring the skill with which the black man moved his head and torso yet kept his balance, almost without putting his hands on the window glass or frames. He obviously knew something about burglar alarms.

The African jumped down from the window and moved out of the picture. Finnerty did not think he was a burglar. Besides, he was sure that he knew who the boy was and why he had come here by dark of night. At his wife's insistence, he had paid for the Nigerian's funeral; he had even attended the burial. But he had not gone close to the graveside nor spoken to any of the mourners, and he would not recognize Shad's brother if he ever saw him again. Yet he knew that he was looking at him now.

He had not expected this development, but he would deal with it.

Having glanced perfunctorily into one or two other rooms, Finnerty went out by the kitchen door and walked to the end of the garden. As he expected, the front and back doors of the studio were securely locked and showed no signs of being tampered with. But as soon as he rounded the corner to the back of the building, he noticed how the fading daffodils under the kitchen window had been slightly trampled. Coming closer, he could see, even from the outside, the slight deposit of garden soil left on the inner window ledge by somebody clambering into the studio through that window.

He walked swiftly back to the front of the studio and let himself in with his key. Slowly, and with cold patience, he reconstructed Jude's visit to the dacha. There was the still-moist potted plants that the boy had watered while trying to calm himself down, the swipe of dust off the window ledge in the same area, a solitary tissue in one of the otherwise empty trash cans, the raised lavatory seat in the bathroom, suggesting a male presence in a rest room which, he was sure, nobody except his wife had ever used before now.

It was clear, too, that somebody had worked at the desk—and by night, because the lamp was pulled right into the center of the table. He found in a drawer the writing pad from which pages had been inexpertly detached. No way would his wife have made, and still less have left, those jagged edges. He looked, last of all, at the bookshelves. His instinct had been to start there, but he had disciplined himself to arrive at that point only at the end of a painstaking process of reconstruction, driven ineluctably by the evidence.

His methodical patience was rewarded. The first of the five volumes on *The Image of the Black in Western Art*, he noted with a sardonic smile, had actually been replaced on its shelf back to front, the spine inward to the wall, the page edges facing outward. This was the work of a hasty hand which, unnerved by the clash of eros and the screeches of an angry owl, had fumbled to be rid of the ill-starred volume. Of course Finnerty knew nothing about eros and the owl. What he did know was that his fastidious wife would no more replace a book that way on a shelf than she would chew tobacco and spit it on the floor.

The next volume, he saw, was out of sequence. This was the one he needed to know about. He took it in hand carefully. The back flap of the dust cover had slipped its moorings and had folded in neatly under the dust cover itself and outside the board. Not major, certainly, but unlike his wife nonetheless.

The book opened effortlessly at the most provocative of the black leg illustrations, the one of the sixteenth-century Valladolid altarpiece panel depicting the black boy sobbing on the floor while the "saintly doctors" impassively attached his amputated leg to the rich white man on his comfortable bed. The reason why the book opened at this place was that two blank A4 ruled sheets had been left between the pages. A quick comparison between these pages and the writing pad in the desk drawer showed that the two blank pages were what remained of five that had been torn out together from that pad. All five had left the same jagged remnant on the pad corresponding exactly with the indentations at the top of the two surviving pages. The obvious conclusion was that whoever had had this book in hand had made and taken away three pages of notes, leaving behind two blank pages, unintentionally marking the place in the book where the writer had been working.

The two pages in Finnerty's hand were still partially stuck together at the top by the glue which had originally attached them to the pad. It seemed clear that the note taker had torn off all five pages together and had used them as a minipad, detaching each individual page as it was filled with writing. It could also be seen that the writer had leaned heavily on his Biro, at least in some places, leaving some quite deep score marks on the unused pages. Most notably, toward the bottom of both sheets, there was the imprint of half a dozen words written in capital letters, which had been almost etched into the page. Even on the bottom copy Finnerty had no problem reading the first five words:

THE HOLY PHYSICIANS EAT SHIT!

"Eat shit" was not an expression Mr. Finnerty was familiar with. He admired its concise vividness and filed it away mentally for use on appropriate occasions, which, he was quite sure, would not be lacking. In the meantime he conjectured that it could well be an African turn of phrase, and so another indication of who might have come calling when no one was there to receive them.

The virulent tenor of the words was quite clear—especially as they were almost carved into the table. They expressed angry and contemptuous rejection of something that somebody else has said or done. This final detail drew together all the threads of what he had been painstakingly reconstructing for the last hour and a half. Mr. Finnerty took it all very personally.

Driving back to Rathgar, Finnerty considered his position. The black man clearly knew much more than was good for him. On the other hand, he did not seem to have drawn all the conclusions or to have shared his knowledge with the police. If the Gardaí had been alerted, they would have been on top of Finnerty at once, looking for his wife and demanding explanations. There was no time to lose.

Mr. Finnerty watched his own mind with clinical detachment, an impartial yet fervently admiring observer—which was not a contradiction, he felt, because his mind was, objectively, inescapably, admirable. His mind was cool, crystal clear, and calculating. If he was mad, his madness was, in fact, a higher form of genius. He had no doubt about that. He felt now, not so much in danger, as dangerous. He lifted his head to look at his face in the rearview mirror. It was entirely satisfactory, as he had expected it to be: grim-set, white-hard, the eyes avid, with the steel glint of a wild beast that sees the hunter cornered and off his guard.

Jim Quilligan and Molly Power had done their best with Professor Ogogie's two suggestions. After prolonged telephone conversations with British police officers, who were the soul of courtesy as always, Molly had spent a total of nine hours online researching the burgeoning world of cults and rituals, especially those given to offing people, or parts of people. Try as she might, she could not imagine any of them prospering on Irish soil.

"Ireland is too wet, or too something, for this sort of thing. Maybe we are still too Christian, or too lazy, whatever. We just don't do this stuff."

"So it must be something the Africans brought in in their own baggage?"

"I don't know, Jan-Hein. All I know is that we are a month into this investigation, and we know precisely nothing."

"Lighten up, sweetheart, and come away from that bloody computer. You will end up with google eyes and a hump on your back."

"Have you a better idea than the *bloody* computer?"

"Yes, I have," he said.

"What?"

"Me."

Quilligan was feeling equally frustrated and more than a little foolish. He had taken on the second area mentioned by Professor Ogogie—the student world—and had conscientiously gone on a tour of all the chaplains in three Dublin universities and in several of the institutes, as well. He chose the chaplains as people who would have their ears close to the ground. Everywhere he was met with the same mixture of courtesy and incredulity. They were not buying it.

Most of the chaplains had come across a little bit of ouija

board, some interest in horoscopes, astrology, or tarot cards, and even a few self-proclaimed witches. There was some antiquarian interest in Maud Gonne McBride, W. B. Yeats, and Aleister Crowley—affectionately known, to himself mostly, as the Great Beast and the Most Evil Man on Earth. There were also a number of zany creatures who combined muddle-headed ecology with vaguely druidic theology. These went romping around the countryside at unusual hours, dressed in lady's night attire and Wellington boots. Quilligan doubted that they were impaling farmers with pitchforks, like the American students in the novel Ogogie had mentioned.

At a joint session at Trinity College Dublin—which was founded by Queen Elizabeth I, who is rather differently remembered by different sections of the Irish population—the Rev. Mr. Winterbottom attempted an evaluation of these various student activities:

"Inspector, none of these people would harm a fly, though they do sometimes harm themselves."

"Ah, yes," agreed Father Smithwick, shaking his head sadly, "the druids *are* rather inclined to fall into bog holes."

"Indeed!" commented the imam, whom the others sometimes suspected of pulling their ecclesiastical legs, "all this blind faith is a bad idea!"

Quilligan did meet one reverend gentleman who was quite convinced that the Harry Potter books were to blame for the whole thing.

"All this harping on magic, Inspector! It is having a very bad effect on our young people. I don't doubt that some of them are dipping into black magic."

"Do you believe in magic, Reverend?"

The tortuous and torturous answer to this question was still going on long after Quilligan had gone home to his supper.

Penelope Finnerty had gone away. People presumed that she had gone abroad. Those who thought they knew said the Swiss Alps, because that is what she had told somebody who could be relied on to repeat it to everybody else. In fact she was on an island off West Cork, in a holiday cottage lent by a close friend, and alone because she wanted to think. Penelope had a lot to think about.

Her childless marriage to Patrick Finnerty had effectively ended two decades before, when she woke up on the morning of their tenth wedding anniversary with the portentous expression, "pronounced dead," inexplicably on her lips. She was as wholly surprised as she was suddenly convinced: her marriage to Patrick Finnerty was indeed finished. This, it would seem to her for ever afterward, had been a blinding flash of the obvious.

There had been no major incident, no flagrant infidelity, no furious rows. Her husband did not behave badly. He did not drink excessively. He did not chase women or boys, expect kinky sex, beat her, fail to provide for her needs, or even for her not inconsiderable wants. He did not complain about her cooking, her clothes, her friends, her painting, or anything else. It was just that he seemed to have forgotten who she was, what she was doing in his house, or even that she actually existed. He sometimes stayed away from the house for days on end without explanation. When he was there, he rarely spoke to her except in the most superficial way. He *did* sex on automatic pilot about as often and as fervently as he cut his toenails: she felt curiously in the way on these occasions, as if he would do better without her.

Burying the dead, as a random occurrence, is one of the corporal works of mercy. As a way of life, it is a bit of a conversation stopper. Undertakers' wives, like the spouses of public hangmen, probably prefer not to talk about what their husbands do. No doubt this, too, had something to do with Patrick and Penelope Finnerty drifting apart. He could hardly brighten up their soirees together with lively accounts of his daily activities. There are limits to the number of times one can lead off with: *A funny thing happened on the way to the crematorium.*

Penelope, in fact, knew little about what her husband did. She had rarely visited the Rathgar funeral home, where he had his headquarters, and had never been in any of his other three premises. She had nonetheless become gradually aware that Patrick, who had always wanted to be a doctor, was dabbling in some sort of shady pathology. She knew that when he was building the Rathgar complex, he had designed a special unit for himself, linked to the main building by a corridor which he normally used, but having also an independent entrance from the outside. This unit comprised, as well as his office, a small flat where he often spent his nights, and a surgical theater equipped with two or more refrigeration cubicles where corpses could be preserved for long periods. These facilities were quite separate from the state-of-the-art installations used by his staff in the main building of the funeral home.

Although she knew few of the people employed by her husband, she did sometimes get disquieting vibes from that quarter. She was aware that several good people had left him, been dismissed, or been transferred from Rathgar to one of his satellite units. On one occasion she had received a highly illiterate and almost illegible letter from one of the cleaning women at Rathgar who complained—how could she forget the spontaneous alliteration—that her husband was "cutting capers with corpses." To this indictment was added the phrase, "and him a nigger." At the time Penelope had understood this last bit as an uncomplimentary reference to her husband's rather swarthy appearance. In the light of recent events, she now wondered if it had not meant that one of the corpses, probably the most recent one, had been a black man. At the time she did nothing, persuading herself that the woman was obviously half-witted and unable to understand some of the clever things that morticians had to do. For the thousandth time, Penelope asked herself now whether Shad might still be alive if she had blown the whistle on receipt of that letter.

Then there had been the thing about the book. On one of his rare visits to her studio, Patrick had been sorting through her library while she worked away at her potter's wheel. He had come across the Miracle of the Black Leg series of paintings and the learned articles about Saints Cosmas and Damian and the Golden Legend. She would not forget that day. It was one of the very few occasions when she had seen him visibly excited about anything. He talked volubly about it: Did she think it was possible to graft somebody's leg onto somebody else? Would the mixture of race, black onto white, make it more or less likely to succeed? If it was a miracle, did she think that such miracles still happened?

Penelope herself had no interest in the topic, but it was such a novel experience to see him animated and so eager to talk that she had humored him and gone along with his enthusiasm. He had taken the book up to the house with him, where he had read and reread it several times over the next few days. When he gave it back, she knew that he had actually procured his own copy through one of the secondhand book sites online. He had also bought a modern translation of the book *The Golden Legend*. She had seen both books coming in the post and had been sufficiently curious to check what they were while her husband was taking his shower.

Sitting in the soft young grass and fragrant wildflowers of early summer on the bluff headland of her island retreat, Penelope looked out over the green Atlantic sighing gently beneath her, sparkling away to the west in the rays of the setting sun. A hundred yards from the shore, a seal was sitting bolt upright in the water, observing her attentively. The beauty, the serenity, the intentness, all invited her to healing and to wholeness, if only she could face the truth, if only she would acknowledge it, at least to herself. This, she realized, was what she had come here to do.

She confessed to herself that, from the time of that incident about the book, which was six or seven years ago, she had known that there was something seriously wrong. It was from then on that Patrick had become less and less present in the house and more and more withdrawn from her, even when he was there. She would also have to say that, if she had been asked any night during that time where she thought he was, she could not have replied truthfully that he was womanizing or drinking. She would have feared that he was in his laboratory, or his surgical theater, or whatever he called it. What he might be doing there, she preferred not to know. But she *did* know: she knew that he was messing with bodies. And she knew that this was wrong.

When Shad was murdered in the horrible way that he was, she did think of those fables about saints and severed legs, and she did remember Patrick's fascination with those paintings. But her husband had never been violent with her and she found it hard to believe that he would ever injure a living person—whatever he might be doing to corpses in his den. Patrick had met Shad a few times. He had even driven him back to town once or twice after modeling sessions. They probably had nothing to say to each other on these occasions, but she could not imagine that Patrick would ever want to harm anyone so gentle and guileless as Shad.

He had been very good about the funeral, laying on his best staff, vehicles, and equipment, and he had even accompanied her to the burial, although he did decline to attend the Mass or to meet the family.

The father confessor seal was watching her intently, from much closer in to the shore, his head and upper body held high in the water, his stern black eye fixed unwaveringly upon her. He was so near now that she could see his mustache bristle in the golden rays of a sun still setting in these western isles, when it was already night over Europe and even on the east coast of Ireland. She must face up now to the most difficult bit. Wasn't this where she had really failed?

It was about six weeks after Shad's funeral. There had been a scare in the media about some nasty bacteria in frozen meat. Everybody was being urged to check their freezers for listed packing numbers on certain brands. She had dutifully been through her kitchen freezer and found nothing to worry about. Then she thought of the garage freezer, which was for long-term storage and seldom opened during the summer months, when she routinely barbecued fresh meat on the patio. There was really no need to check this freezer because whatever was in it had been in there since before the infected consignment had come on the market.

She checked it all the same, with the unexpected result that, next day, she found herself destroying almost the entire contents of the cabinet and having the freezer itself removed, as well. She retained only one item, which she had found wedged between the chickens and the turkeys. This was a transparent freezer bag containing Shad's severed foot. In the very second that she saw it, she knew beyond the slightest doubt that it had to be Shad's.

She had almost fainted with the shock, sinking to the ground, supporting herself against the freezer with one hand, clutching the sad remnant to her breast with the other. Utterly stunned, she felt no revulsion for what she held to her heart, only infinite sorrow, tenderness, pity, and deep shame. How unbearably sad it was, so small, so pale for one who had been so dazzlingly black, so naked and defenseless. How beautiful, too, it was, so light, with its fine-boned toes, as long as a child's fingers, the nails so clean and perfectly formed, each with its tiny, flawless mother-of-pearl half-moon.

She had sat there on the ground for a long time, silent at first, then sobbing as if her heart would break.

"Shad, oh Shad, what have we done to you?"

At last she stood up. She went upstairs and took her most beautiful silk headscarf from her wardrobe. She took her jewelry case and emptied the contents out on her bed. She came downstairs again, wrapped the limb in her scarf, coaxed it into the jewelry box. She dug a little grave in the garden near to her studio and buried Shad's poor remains.

She could not bear to see him or to speak to him. For three days she agonized about what to do. Then, fatuously, as it seemed even to herself, she sent him an e-mail to his private address:

I have found what you hid in the garage. I never want to see you again, never! Do not ring, I will not talk to you. I will stay away from the house all day on Friday. Come and take what you want. Then never again. If you come near me, I will go straight to the police and tell them everything.

On the island, she admitted to herself that the last sentence was, in fact, a sort of promise that she would not go to the police, not give him away, provided that he left her alone. She knew that this was how he would interpret it. She knew, too, that he would stay away, at least for now, perhaps for several months. That would give her space. She needed that space to work out what she had to do.

She had not been surprised that her husband had accepted his sentence of banishment with indifference. What had appalled her was the extent of that indifference. He had not even replied to her e-mail. No word of explanation, no protest of innocence. He had simply come on the Friday, as she had demanded, and removed, if not everything, a nonetheless significant quantity of his personal possessions.

A week later, he had sent her an impersonal but pleasantly worded e-mail setting out practical arrangements to do with property and finance. Everything he suggested seemed sensible and even generous. She had replied acknowledging that fact and mentioning that she would be leaving for West Cork for an indefinite period. There was a short reply: "Fine; I'll keep an eye!" Neither of his e-mails was signed.

One morning as she walked the sandy beach forming the lee shore of her island, two puzzling questions concerning Shad's death suddenly yielded to the same simple answer. Why had the boy been so perfunctorily dumped in a place which had obviously not been carefully preselected and where, according to the newspapers, the chances were high that the body would be found sooner rather than later? The second question, which concerned her more immediately, was what had possessed Patrick to bring the severed limb back to her house and to put it in her freezer—when he had state-of-the art facilities in his Rathgar funeral home?

But exactly! She remembered now that there had been a major emergency one night around that time when the entire refrigeration system in Rathgar had collapsed. They had had to remove four or five bodies urgently to other funeral homes in the small hours of the morning. If it should turn out, as she was now sure it would, that this was the night when Shad disappeared, the answer to the two questions became gruesomely clear:

Finnerty is stranded in the middle of the night with a foot that he has just amputated and with a victim from whom he intends to take further organs, then or later, and who, in either case, is not intended to survive the night. Suddenly, he finds himself without refrigeration facilities and about to be invaded and discovered by a full-scale emergency crew with a body he cannot account for. What does he do? He seizes the biggest car to hand, a funeral car perhaps, rather than his personal vehicle, and drives in haste to the Dublin Mountains where he dumps the dying man—to whom he may even have administered a lethal dose of anesthetic to finish him off.

Then, so that he will not lose everything—the utter cold-bloodedness of it!—he brings the severed foot of his victim back to her house and hides it in her freezer.

It was dark now except for a faint afterglow on the western horizon and the rhythmic shafting of the night by the fiery lance of the Fastnet lighthouse. Penelope opened her eyes to the central issue. It was not just a question of whether or not her husband should be punished for what he had done to Shad. Even less important was what, in his demented mind, he thought or imagined he was achieving by his horrible experiments. The urgent necessity was to know whether the refrigeration cubicles in his private quarters were intended for people who came into his hands, not dead but alive. Was there any way of knowing how often he had done this thing before? Most important of all was to make absolutely sure that he would never do it again. She should have faced this long ago. She would leave for Dublin tomorrow.

Quilligan was sitting at home the same evening explaining Nigeria, and indeed the rest of Africa, to his next-door neighbors. Tim, his eldest, put his head around the door.

"Dad, President Mumbojumbo on the blower for you."

"Who?"

"One of your African pals anyhow. It's got to be a president at least, if he is ringing *you* up."

"Piss off, and thanks! Excuse, folks, this could be something."

It was.

"Inspector, this is Jude. Miss Molly give me your number of telephone in case I am sometime wanting to say something."

"Yes, Jude, hello. What is it?"

"Can I see you tomorrow? I want to tell you all the things I know about Shad's death."

"Jude, I am very glad to hear this. And I, in my turn, will tell you all that I know, which is not much. I can only hope that you know more than I do. Do you?"

"I think so."

"Do you know who killed Shad?"

There was a pause. Then Jude said again,

"I think so."

"Who?"

Another pause.

"Please, Inspector, can we *not* talk this time? It is ten o'clock now. We are finish our work in the restaurant. I want to sit down and write out the entire things I know. If we start palaver now, I will mix up every this thing."

"Okay, Jude. I understand. Write everything down very carefully. So what time tomorrow? If I come to your place at, say, ten o'clock, how about that?"

"Is good!"

CHAPTER THIRTEEN

Pita was out for the count. The motorbike excursion to Rathgar, the hours of high-alert waiting, the exhilaration of finding "his man" after so much patience and such a bitter disappointment some weeks before, the excitement of knowing that Jude was even now drawing all the threads together and that Shad's murderer would soon be captured—it was too much for one day. He had tried to stay with Jude when he sat down to write, but he was falling asleep on his feet. Besides, he sensed that Jude needed to be alone to think out what he wanted to say and to get it down on paper. He slipped away and was soon fast asleep on his favorite bench behind the table in the corner.

He had slept for perhaps an hour. Vaguely, as if in a dream, he became aware that Jude was speaking on the telephone. Scraps of phrases floated in and out of his dreams, half registering with him, as he slipped in and out of consciousness.

"You trapped Shad the same way . . . what could you tell me that I don't know? . . . expect me to believe that . . . of course, I want to know . . . of course, I want him to be caught . . . well, yes . . . is that really true? . . . your own wife! . . . in the car, yes . . . I no go in any house . . ."

Pita drifted back to sleep. Time passed. Suddenly he was wide awake, his body tingling with a sense of danger, his heart beating faster—before his mind knew why. The street door had just closed. He sat bolt upright, rolled off his bench onto the floor. Something was wrong, very wrong.

"Jude!"

He ran to the door and opened it.

"Jude, don't go!"

He could see him, already fifty yards away, walking swiftly, west on Parnell Street. Shreds of that half-heard telephone conversation were coming back to him, like fragments of a nightmare.

"*Jude!*" he screamed.

Jude heard him. He turned and waved.

"Go back, Pita; it is all right." He turned and continued walking rapidly.

"*No, Jude, no! Don't go! I beg!*"

He began to run after him, then suddenly realized that he was barefoot and wearing only an undershirt and boxer shorts. He ran back to the retaurant, threw on his clothes, searched for his shoes, remembered that they had gotten wet during the day. Margot had put them somewhere to dry. *Where? Where?* He hunted frantically, the stove, the airing cupboard, the boiler. All he could find was an old pair of backless sandals, flip-flops. He pulled off his socks again, jabbed the V-straps between his toes, and ran out the door.

Jude had disappeared from view. Which way to turn? Toward the river? Yes, surely: that was the way Shad had gone, the night that *he* died. He turned, ran up Parnell Street, left into Moore Street, across Henry Street, on into Abbey Street, where he stopped.

Okay, yes, he thought, but what then? I get to the river, what then? What am I doing? Where am I going? Think, you little shit! *Think!* You are runing around like a headless chicken. *Think!*

He thought like he had never thought before. He wished he was religious, like Shad and Jude, so that he could pray. But who would he pray to? He only knew Ijaw Delta gods. They were great and terrible, and he was afraid of them. Who was he to talk to those gods? He was only nobody at all. Anyhow Delta gods would have no power to do anything in this place. He tried to pray to Jude's God. Yes, he even gave him a capital g in his mind. Gods like to be flattered: he knew that much.

Please, Jude's God, please! he implored silently. This is *urgent!* Excuse me saying it, but you screwed up rightly on Shad. Don't let Jude go that same way, please, *I beg!* Jude is very terrific man. If you let him go die now, like this way again, you are *shit god!* Oh! Excuse me, but *fuckfuckfuck!* Kill *me,* if you must kill someone, but *save Jude!* Tell me, what will I do? Which way will I turn? *Look now!* I am only small, but I am *trying!*—and I am *crying!*

It was true: he was crying. He stood at the corner of Abbey Street, cold, alone, waiting on Jude's God. But, as the Holy Bible says, there was silence in heaven. Nothing happened. He turned slowly and walked back to the restaurant, head down, shoulders drooping.

What is it about me? he wondered. Everybody who love me go die. My mammy go die, my sister and my brother go die, Shad go die—and now Jude: must he go die, too? I am worth nothing. I bring only sorrow and bad fortune to person.

He felt tired and sick. He went into the restaurant, sat at a table, dropped his head on his hands, and slept for very grief.

Patrick Finnerty smiled at his good fortune, and even more at his own sheer genius. It was by good fortune that he had gotten to the boy just in time. The fool had not yet told anyone about his discoveries in Penelope's studio, but he was planning to tell the police about them the very next day. Such neat timing! He, Patrick Finnerty, would now see to it that the nigger would never tell anybody anything.

It was not all luck, of course. It was by his own superior intelligence that he had been able, not only to reconstruct the boy's movements on the night when he visited Foxrock, but also to estimate fairly exactly how much he had discovered during that visit. Finnerty had just had the satisfaction of having all of his deductions confirmed on the telephone by Jude himself.

The nigger had been extremely hostile during that conversation. He had been downright insolent. But Finnerty had kept his cool. He had even congratulated the little shit on how much he had been able to find out. To be fair, he had done very well. Finnerty could not deny: he was impressed. But that was precisely why he was so dangerous. It was essential to destroy him *tonight,* before he got a chance to talk to the police or to confront Penelope with all that he knew.

That, of course, had been his master play, devised at the spur of the moment and executed flawlessly. Penelope! To get his hands on Jude, he had blamed his wife for everything. He had pretended that it was only by following Jude's trail from the main house to the studio that he had been led from what had seemed like an ordinary burglary to the awful secret of the art books and "the miracle of the severed leg." He had never heard of this before, he claimed, and he had been "utterly appalled." With tears in his voice, he described to Jude his anger and his heartbreak to discover his wife's terrible secret, and what her cruel and depraved fascination with Shad had really been all about.

Jude, who, it seemed, had met his wife and liked her, had put up a fight against this interpretation, and Finnerty had had to do some nimble footwork.

"But it was *you* who brought Shad away that night—I know. I have a witness."

There was a fractional pause. (A witness. *Shit!* Who?)

"Yes, I did, I admit it. I collected him—in Temple Bar—to bring him out to my wife. She wanted to paint him. But this wasn't the first time I had done that for her. She said that she would drive him back herself, as I had business in town that night."

"But Shad's chaplet—his rosary beads—which fell off his neck, was found in the back of one of your big black funeral cars. He was in one of those cars the night he died."

"There must be some mistake."

"There is *no* mistake. Shad wore that chaplet around his neck, day and night. It was missing when he was brought to the hospital, and it was found under the seat of your car on the day of his burial."

There was a longer pause. Then:

"Ah, now I remember. That night I took my wife's car into town. It is smaller and easy to park. So she had my car. She must have driven Shad in it, later . . ."

"Your car is a big *green* car: I am talking about a big *black* funeral car."

Another pause. (How does the litle prick know all this stuff about my cars?)

"Ah, yes. My green car was in for servicing. You are quite right.

I had one of the funeral cars that night. So if this rosary beads thing was found in that car, it must have fallen off when . . . when my wife was . . ."

"Did you tell the police all this? Did you tell them that you had driven Shad that night?" Jude asked.

"The police never came near me, never asked me any questions. The only contact with them was when *I* approached *them*, to offer to do your brother's funeral—for *free!*"

"But they were asking everybody who knew anything to—"

"Look, Jude, I had no idea at the time that my information was significant. As far as I knew, I had collected Shad and my wife had left him safely back at the restaurant *before* the terrible events of that night began to happen. Whatever tragedy befell Shad came later. That is what I believed—until I saw that horrible book that my wife had on her shelf and that you yourself led me to. Listen, I don't want to talk about all this on the telephone. Will you come and talk to me? Ten minutes will be enough. I have something really important to tell you about all this."

"I am not going to your house. No way!"

"You don't have to. I am in the city. I don't want to come to your place, and you don't want to come to mine. Fair enough. Come and meet me on neutral ground. I'll park on Parnell Square West. That is right beside you. I'll be there in twenty minutes time. Sit in the car with me for ten minutes. I will tell you something you really need to know before you talk to the police tomorrow.

"Look, Jude, this is not easy for me, either. Make the effort, boy, will you, *for Shad's sake!*"

———

Twenty minutes later Jude went, for Shad's sake. Pita came running after him, but he shouted to him to go back. It was about eleven o'clock at night. Finnerty was waiting for him. He was not in his green car, nor was it one of the big funeral limos. Some kind of medium-size Ford, Jude thought, inconspicuous. Finnerty got out and shook hands with him. Jude gave his hand reluctantly.

"This will not take long. Let us sit in the back together. That way, you can be sure: I will not drive off suddenly, taking you prisoner."

He laughed engagingly—at least he thought it was engaging. Jude almost turned on his heel and walked away.

"We can talk out here."

"Please, Jude—you have been so good—this is very private."

He held the door open. Jude got in. He slid across and made sure that his door was unlocked. Finnerty got in beside him. He started talking volubly, about Shad and his wife, about tragedy and Nigeria, about Dublin and almost anything at random. Jude could not see where this monologue was going. It was an absurd mishmash of disconnected items. There was no sign of any big revelation, no vital issue that made this crouching furtively together on the backseat of a car in the middle of the night either necessary or useful.

Besides, Jude was distracted from what Finnerty was saying. As he talked, the undertaker was rummaging in the dark with something he had taken out of his pocket. Jude peered at it suspiciously. It looked like a shallow tin box. Was the man going to smoke? He hoped not. Cigarette smoke in a confined space made him sick. Finnerty took something from the tin, which he held out awkwardly, away from himself. There was a strange sweet smell. Suddenly Finnerty rolled over, right on top of him. Jude was utterly startled. Was the man trying to sex him or to kill him? It had to be one or the other. He struggled, but the pad was already firmly over his mouth and nose. Finnerty was holding him now at arm's length, crushing his head back against the side window of the car.

"Shad!" he gasped once through the vaporizing chloroform, and was gone.

Finnerty made sure of him with an injection, rolled him onto the floor of the car where he covered him with a blanket. Then he climbed into the front seat and drove off.

Pita lifted his head. He was looking straight at the shoes he could not find earlier. They were tucked in under the sideboard. He took it as a sign. He jumped up, ran over, and put them on. They were bone dry. A second sign. It was nearly midnight. He ran upstairs and looked in Jude's room. He had not returned. That was serious, but Pita felt that some of his strength and his courage had come back. That was a third sign.

I *will* find him . . . where will I go? I will go where the enemy is. If Jude is there, I will save him. If he is not there, he is safe.

He liked these answers, which seemed to come from somewhere strong and resolute within himself. He ran upstairs again, grabbed what he needed, came down, and slipped out quickly. "Who knows," he said out loud, "I might meet a crocodile!" He stopped outside Tunde's snooker hall, then remembered: Tunde had gone to some place called Kildare to buy a bigger billiard table. He would not be back until after the auction next day. No hope of his motorbike.

"I go trek!" Pita said to nobody.

It would be a very long way on foot, but he started walking. Down to the river. The tide was out. He smelled fish, or something to make him think of the delta and of home. He crossed the water at Capel Street Bridge, got lost, found himself at city hall.

"Where is this place? Where is the first church?" He wandered randomly up to his right. "*Eheh!*" There it was.

He passed Christ Curch, started up High Street, realized his mistake, went back to the cathedral and turned right, into Nicholas Street. On down to the second church, St. Patrick's Cathedral. He had walked a lot and was getting tired. It was not just the walking, it was the constant anxiety about being on the right road. He had been this way twice already today, going and coming to Rathgar; but high speed on the back of a motorcycle by daylight and foot slogging alone after midnight were two very different experiences.

Finnerty drew up before the pillared gateway to the grounds of his funeral home. There was an electronically controlled barrier in place at night after ten o'clock, when the last mourners were expected to leave. He used his zapper and drove through. Bypassing his reserved parking place at the main entrance, he continued down the south side of the buildings until he came to the pentagonal unit that stood apart from the rest of the complex behind its own landscaped screen of shrubbery and hedges. Here he had his office, his modest three-room flat, and his private "research area," as he called it.

"Paddy's Pagoda" as his employees irreverently called the whole structure, was linked to the funeral home by fifteen yards of carpeted corridor that went nowhere else and served no other purpose. It was an inflexible rule in the business that nobody came down that corridor uninvited. Employees communicated with their boss by interphone and e-mail, or face to face if they were lucky enough to catch him on his way through the main building. Many, perhaps most, had never been as far as his office: very few, with the exception of hand-picked cleaning staff, had ever been into his living quarters.

Finnerty was a respected funeral director. A good administrator, with a keen eye for the market, he wisely left the highly sensitive work of human contact with the bereaved to gentler, more empathetic persons than himself. Whatever about his mediocre talent for getting on nicely with the living, he succeeded marvelously well with the dead. A superb embalmer in even the most difficult cases, he had a skill bordering on genius for the cosmetic side of the business. To speak plainly, he could make even the most tragically disfigured corpse look passable. It was not work that he did routinely. As he put it, rather crudely, you don't buy a dog and bark yourself, but he could be called upon in difficult cases.

When asked to do such work, Finnerty generally operated in the central theater or "laboratory," as they called it, which had state-of-the-art equipment. Sometimes, for no apparent reason, he would decide to transfer a "patient" to his own much smaller theater in the pagoda. More mysteriously, he had done this also with a number of corpses where his help had *not* been requested and where there was no obvious reason to invoke it. On those occasions, he would just appear in the laboratory and choose a cadaver according to some strange criteria of his own. There were still other cases where, it was known, corpses had been delivered directly to the pagoda from outside, without any paperwork passing through the central office.

In many instances, the strangest feature of Finnerty's interventions was that when the "patient" was eventually returned to the main building for onward processing toward the grave or crematory, he or she arrived washed, dressed, casketed, and fully ready for wake, funeral service, and/or burial. This was puzzling because there was no need for it. The fine points of casketing do require an experienced hand, but the routine chores of washing and dressing corpses, though also requiring training and skill, are not usually complicated. What is mostly needed, especially for dressing a corpse, is physical strength. The job would normally be done by one or even two younger persons. So why was Finnerty doing this simple and strenuous work himself?

There could be no avoiding the conclusion that Finnerty did not want people to see what he was doing down in the pagoda or to examine too closely the results of those procedures.

There were other disturbing factors. A medical student who had a holiday job at the funeral home was perturbed to see a prescription, made out to Finnerty, for a large quantity of potassium chloride. This is a chemical which, in tiny amounts, is beneficial and even necessary to the electrical conduction that makes muscles and nerves work. It is regularly used in the treatment of patients who are severely dehydrated or debilitated. But in concentrated form, potassium chloride, administered intravenously, would cause cardiac arrest within seconds. Its only uses that this medical student had ever heard of were in assisted suicides and in executions by lethal injection. He could think of no legitimate use for this bottle in a mortician's business. He had asked one of Finnerty's assistants about it, and lost his job two days later.

The most alarming rumor circulating in the funeral home, behind sanitarily gloved hands, was that Finnerty had received a complaint from one of the Dublin crematories, alleging that, on two occasions, cremated remains of cadavers emanating from the Rathgar funeral home were found to contain more bones than a single corpse could account for. It was not suggested that there had been more than one body in any casket, but that, on at least these two occasions, a severed body part with a bone of sufficient size to survive incineration had been concealed in the coffin of another person. In both cases, it was whispered, the casket had been one that had emerged from Paddy's Pagoda.

Finnerty pulled up at the rear of his pagoda, out of vision of anybody in the main building or in the parking lot. He checked on Jude and found him still deeply unconscious. Letting himself in, he went down the corridor toward the laboratory where he had seen a light as he drove in. He did not want people around this night.

Nellie Moynihan was working on a smashed face. Finnerty summed up the situation at a glance. She was going well, but it would take another two hours at least, two hours that she could not have. He wanted Jude dead, selected organs removed, and the body safely stowed or disposed of. It could all be done, but he needed time and privacy.

"That's a bad one you have there, Nellie."

"It is, Paddy, but I'll manage."

"No, I'm afraid not. Look at those cheekbones."

"You should have seen them an hour ago. I can lift them all right. It just takes time."

"No, I'm telling you, it won't work—especially not with that kind of skin. She will be black and blue."

"Sure, we can fix that."

"I said no! Veil the face. We'll say it was the best we could do in the circumstances. Put her away, and go home."

Nellie looked up, astonished both by the sudden sharpness of tone and by the decision, which she knew in her heart was wrong and totally contrary to Finnerty's own professional standards. But you did not argue with Finnerty.

"Very well, sir."

He did a bad sketch of a smile, said good night, and went back the way he had come.

Pita's earlier burst of courage and energy was ebbing fast. He had been walking for more than an hour, had lost his way three times, and was dog tired. He was also fighting a nauseous combination of rising and sinking emotions, dejection that he had been too long on the road, and panic that, after all his sweat and labor, he would find nothing when he got there but a dark and derelict building and, worst of all, that even now Jude was lying dead in some ditch or drain on the Dublin Mountains. Then, just when he felt tears stinging at his eyes again, he got his lucky break, or his answer to prayer. He found a bicycle.

It was a woman's bicycle, lying half on the sidewalk and half onto the road at Camden Street Lower. It had been "borrowed" in Ballsbridge an hour or two earlier by an inebriated student desirous of reaching his bed. Having got there, or as near as the bicycle could carry him, he had abandoned his mount and continued unsteadily on his way. Pita did not doubt that this bicycle had fallen from heaven, dispatched by Jude's God who, if slow off the mark, was at last beginning to get his act together. He sprang to the saddle and shot out into the middle of the road, putting the heart across the 1:30 A.M. traffic of homeward-bound topers.

The seat was high for his short legs, so a lot of the time he had to cycle standing on the pedals. There was some sort of gear arrangement but, as he had never seen one on the big black bicycles that are standard in his own country, he ignored it. Fortunately the brakes were good.

His luck had certainly changed because, soon afterward, he came to the small river, the Grand Canal, which he had been seeking anxiously for some time, like a nineteenth-century explorer hunting for the source of the Nile. He crossed over the humpback bridge, onto the Ranelagh Road. From there, he knew, it was straight ahead. Alternating pedaling as fast as he could with sitting up briefly to freewheel and rest his weary body, he headed resolutely for Rathgar.

Finnerty dragged Jude's inert body out of the back of his car and hoisted it somehow onto a gurney, which he wheeled through French doors into his private theater. There he cut the clothes off the body with a large scissors, rolled it onto the operating table, and covered it with a sheet. The clothes he stuffed into a plastic refuse sack, to be incinerated next day, leaving one clue less to suggest that Jude had passed this way. He went into his office where he brewed himself a double-strength whiskey punch and sat down.

Finnerty had no need to steady his nerves for what lay ahead: his hand would not shake when it came to wielding a knife. What he did need was to let his strategic thinking catch up with his precipitate action. The first priority had been to take Jude out of circulation. He had done that. The issue now was to decide how much use he could make of his captive before he put him down. He needed to think about that.

His transplant experiments with various organs, though brilliant, of course, had all, or almost all, to be conducted using dead donor and recipient conscripts. The opportunity to work with living tissue was rare, and very tempting when it was offered. It was because he had a willing recipient, somebody sufficiently desperate to try anything, that he had gone out several weeks ago and captured Shad. If everything had gone according to plan, he would have completed that night the greatest experiment of his life, grafting the black man's living foot onto the white woman whose cancerous limb he had amputated ten hours earlier. Meanwhile he could have kept Shad on ice—having killed him humanely, of course—until he had time to take further organs for various useful purposes.

Through no fault of his own, everything had gone disastrously wrong that night because of a wretched power failure. He had just finished a careful amputation when they rang from the laboratory to say that the refrigeration plant had collapsed and that they would have to evacuate all refrigerated units without delay, including his own. He would have been in deep trouble if they had come along and found him with Shad's mutilated body. He had just had time to do some rudimentary suturing, and to get the black man out of the place and away to the nearest dumping ground he could find in a huge hurry.

He had intended to bring some pavulon, a paralyzing agent, to kill the fellow off humanely. But, working under such pressure, he had omitted to do so. He regretted the oversight because, being a gentle person, he would not like anyone, however primitive, to suffer unnecessarily. Another mitigating factor which made him feel better about his forgetfulness was that he had already given the chap a fairly massive dose of sodium thiopental as an anesthetic. He was very surprised to hear afterward that he had woken up from that, even to the point of being able to walk around—or, well, let's say, to *move* around.

Now Finnerty was very tempted to keep Jude alive until he had another suitable recipient for some of his organs because live grafting, and especially of black to white, was the area of his ob-

session. The intended beneficiary of Shad's involuntary organ do-
nations had, unfortunately, passed away the same night as he had
had to dispose of the donor—which is why Finnerty had ended
up hiding the severed limb in his wife's winter freezer. He did not
know when he would next have a sufficiently desperate and willing recipient. He had to be very circumspect about advertising
his willingness to undertake such operations: the medical profes-
sion was notoriously jealous of its exclusive right to experiment
with people.

An alternative strategy would be to sell some of Jude's organs.
Apart from any transplants he might do himself, Finnerty had a
ready market for fresh organs in good condition. But that kind of
deal had to be set up very carefully and carried through with precision timing, so that donor and recipient were perfectly syn-
chronized. This was just not possible in the present case. Jude
had to make his exit that very night, and no recipient had been
suitably prepared. After a second large whiskey punch, he decided that the best he could do in the circumstances would be to
put the nigger down—the potassium chloride would probably be
the best suppressant in this case—having taken whatever organs
he wanted to retain for purely experimental work. He could preserve the rest on ice until he could dispose of it, by incineration if
possible, piecemeal if necessary. He would have plenty of time
for that because nobody would come here looking for Jude. Why
should they?

But somebody *had* come for that very purpose: Pita had just arrived. He stowed his bicycle in the shrubbery, away from the entrance, crawled under the barrier, and ran lightly up to the
darkened funeral home. A quick circuit of the main building es-

tablished that there were no lights burning in there. Having got almost right around, from west, to east, to north, Pita was approaching Paddy's Pagoda from the secluded side. Here he *did* see lights. There were two windows lit up, one directly facing him, on the north side of the building, the other on the next, northwest, plane of the pentagon. He crept up to the nearer window and peeped in.

He watched as Finnerty, dressed in a surgical robe, mask, and gloves, loaded a trolley with some very sinister-looking equipment: long surgical scissors, knives, what looked like an electrical circular saw, swabs, basins, clamps, some kind of pump, and other fearsome gadgets: Pita had no idea what devastation they could be used for. He saw Finnerty fill two syringes with different colored liquids from two bottles and lay them also on his trolley, which he then started to roll toward the door to the next room.

Pita jumped down from the sacks of fertilizer where he had been perched and ran around to the other illuminated window, under which he found an obliging wheelbarrow to stand on. His heart pounded. There was Jude lying flat on his back on an operating table, such as Pita had last seen while, very unwillingly, having his tonsils extracted, without anesthetic, three years earlier in Bomadi. Jude was stretched, his feet toward the window, asleep or dead, but probably not dead—yet—if all that equipment was being assembled for him. *That saw!* This devil was going to cut off Jude's foot—like he had done with Shad—and Jude would die!

Finnerty came in, pushing his loaded trolley to the head of the operating table. He checked Jude's pulse, flicked one of his eyelids up and down with his thumb, then whipped the sheet off his body. Pita was shocked to see that Jude was entirely naked: not that nakedness is a big deal for an African. But in this situation, Jude's nakedness expressed his utter defenselessness, and the extent to which his privacy, his dignity, his physical integrity, and his very life were at the mercy of this monster, who had already murdered Shad.

What should I do? Pita asked himself urgently.

He watched as Finnerty plugged in an electric razor and began shaving the body hair off Jude's abdomen.

What in God's name is he doing that for? he wondered, unfamiliar with this refinement of modern surgery. Was it some sort of sexual perversion, one of these sick things in "western civilization" that Peggy Breen had warned him about after a certain puzzling encounter?

There was worse to come. Finnerty took a vicious-looking knife and began making a surface incision on the stomach. Pita could see the blood pearling as the knife slid down toward the groin. *Enough!* He had to do *something!* He cried out. He struck the double-glazed window with his two fists. Finnerty did not hear it, or if he did, he was distracted by something even more urgent. Jude had begun to move on the table. He was trying to sit up. He was struggling weakly to push this devil out of hell away from him with one arm, while lifting himself up with the other.

Pita's heart was slamming so hard against his windpipe, he thought he would faint or die or go mad. He saw Finnerty smash his fist into Jude's face. Then, holding the African down with one hand, he reached out with the other hand for one of the two syringes on his trolley. He found a vein and jammed the needle in. Jude struggled feebly for a few seconds more, then went limp and fell back flat on the table.

Pita looked around wildly for something—anything. He saw a garden gnome, about a foot and a half high, presiding over a small rockery, three yards from where he stood. He presumed it was a deity of some kind. Well, god or no god, taboo, curse, or damnation—to hell with the lot of it! He leaped down from his wheelbarrow, ran over, and dragged the surly-looking god up in his arms by the head. It was heavy, but he staggered back with the strength of desperation, got himself and the plaster dwarf back up onto the wheelbarrow. Straining every muscle and sinew in his body, he lifted the gnome as high as he could and fell against the window with all his meagre weight.

It was enough. The window smashed in pieces with a great cymbal crash while the gnome fell to the ground inside the room with a thump that rattled the torture tools on Finnerty's trolley and shock-waved the syringe out of his hand and into smithereens all over the floor. Finnerty lifted his head in startled fury. Pita chose immediately his course of action: he *must* get this monster away from Jude, whatever the cost. Sticking his head into the gaping hole in the window, he uttered a great blood-curdling war-cry: "AAAAAIIIAAAAHHH!" which he followed up, at the top of his voice, with his entire if not very extensive repertory of vituperation, malediction, and insult in English:

"Eat shit, you fuckfuck, bastard! Piss in your own well! May crocodile eat your arse for chop!"

Finnerty stared at this apparition, speechless with initial ter-ror, astonishment, then white-hot anger. Thoughts raced through his head: Who was this child? How had he come here? Black, he was with Jude! How could that be? How did he know to be here? Was it a trap? Had Jude double-crossed him? Not possible! You don't send a boy on a man's errand. You don't let something so dangerous run on for so long. A very little time more—and Jude would have been dying or even dead!

He grabbed up the long surgical knife he had been using. Very well, he thought, two niggers would die tonight instead of one! No way could he allow this little shit to get away. Jude could wait. Not enough of the sodium thiopental had gone in to kill him—because of this infuriating interruption—but he would stay asleep for hours to come.

Meanwhile Finnerty would catch this black bastard brat, torture the shit out of him—to find out how much he knew, and who else might know anything. Then he would kill him, and plunder his carcass, too, for body parts. Children's organs were always in great demand—for the operating table—or even for the dining table!

Finnerty had at least one pretty sick—as in weird—customer who regarded the funeral home as a delicatessen.

He ran out through the French doors. Pita was taken by surprise, not reckoning on there being a door so near. He had just time to jump down from his wheelbarrow and swivel it quickly into the path of his furious assailant. Finnerty went down with a crash, blaspheming fluently. Pita ran with all the speed he could muster back the way he had come. He was conscious of a boundary fence, to his left, separating the funeral home grounds from an adjoining property where there seemed to be plenty of cover. He sprang nimbly up and over the chain-link fence, kicking off the frantic hand he felt clawing at his ankle.

At that moment a shrill alarm went berserk back at the funeral home. Finnerty gasped in rage. How had he forgotten the alarm! It was programmed to sound off five minutes after a window breakage, the idea being that if the breakage was accidental, somebody in the house would have time to disarm the siren. Otherwise, and at this very moment, the alert was being signalled to the nearest Garda station, which would immediately contact the closest patrol car. He was fighting on all fronts now. He must kill that child, get back to the pagoda, telephone the police to say it was all a mistake, then get Jude into an icebox—just in case a patrol car did turn up.

Pita, too, heard the alarm. He was not quite sure what it was; but such noise in the night had to be good. It was screaming at people everywhere to come and see what Finnerty was doing. As he darted and flitted from one cover to the next, Pita sensed the rising savage desperation of his pursuer. He knew that he would not survive ten seconds if he let this wild beast near him. Size was his trump card: he could squeeze through places where the big oaf could not follow. Yet, he also knew that he must not escape, he must not run away. His vital task was to risk everything, to engage the enemy, to keep Finnerty busy, to prevent him, by any and every means, from going back to Jude.

But he was worn out. He knew that he could not keep up the effort much longer. To give himself any chance, to give Jude a chance, he must face the final showdown, the shoot-out, while he still had some little bit of energy left. They were in a small grove of young evergreen trees. He could hear Finnerty coming after him, urgently, avidly. This was it! He had done everything that he possibly could. Let this be it, just so. Deliberately, he backed himself against a solid blackthorn hedge. There was nowhere else to run. He was cornered. Here he would make his last stand.

Abruptly, the murderer broke cover fifteen yards below him. As he took in the scene at a glance, a savage smile of triumph twisted his thin, cruel lips. He lifted the knife high above his head and advanced menacingly on the boy.

"Come here to me, you little shit! I'll make you sorry. By Christ, I'll make you sorry!"

Pita trembled, but he stood his ground, foursquare. He turned slowly to face his assailant, a calm, self-disciplined, measured movement. When Finnerty was twelve feet from his quarry, his knife already swooping down, he saw the arrow. A fraction of a second later, it bisected his heart.

CHAPTER FOURTEEN

A PATROL CAR ARRIVED AT THE FUNERAL HOME WITHIN twenty minutes of the alarm sounding. Unable to pass the front gate barrier, the two Gardaí on board, Bill and Sue, left their car at the gate and went walking. Sue spotted the broken window of the pagoda and peeped in. She saw Jude lying there on the operating table and thought he looked yummy. Then she thought how depraved it was to be thinking that way about a corpse, because, naturally, she assumed that anyone lying down in a funeral home had to be dead. Meanwhile Bill, who had gone in by the French doors, noticed that the "corpse" was bleeding through its yummy tummy and breathing through its open mouth. Failing to find anybody else alive anywhere on the campus, they called an ambulance.

Pita watched from the bushes as they wheeled Jude out on a gurney, across the parking lot, and down to the barrier where the ambulance was waiting. He knew that Jude was still alive because they had not covered his face. He was probably still fast asleep, but the relaxed attitude of the attendants seemed to say that he was not in any great danger. Pita bowed his head and, not knowing what to say, thanked Jude's God wordlessly in his heart.

His journey back to the restaurant was mostly downhill, which was merciful but also dangerous, because every time he sat up and freewheeled he started to fall asleep. It was 5:00 A.M. by the time he got there. He dropped the bicycle where he stood, and where it would be "borrowed" again shortly afterward, for the third time in eighteen hours. He let himself in, ate a banana and drank milk, then shut himself into Jude's room, where he knew he would not be disturbed. He lay on the bed and slept for ten hours without stirring.

The police were not long about identifying Jude and connecting what had happened to him with the murder inquiry into the death of his brother. They got in touch with Quilligan. The inspector and Molly Power arrived at St. Vincent's Hospital at 8:00 A.M. to be told that they could not speak to Jude for twenty-four hours. They called Margot, who had presumed that Jude was gone to market. She was very perturbed to hear of his nocturnal adventures. As far as Margot knew, Jude had been alone in the house that night. She had no idea how or when he had gone or been taken to the funeral home in Rathgar. While Quilligan was having this conversation on his cellphone, Molly was driving them to that funeral home, where they were soon hard at work in Paddy's Pagoda, trying to make sense of a trolley loaded with surgical instruments, a broken window, and a garden gnome.

Later in the morning, Nellie Moynihan told the story of her peremptory dismissal from the laboratory the previous night. Toward midday the forensic experts were able to confirm that the contents of the two syringes had been, respectively, sodium thiopental and potassium chloride, in sufficient quantities of either to kill three strong men. The experts also confirmed that neither drug had any legitimate use in a funeral home, and the same remark would apply to several other bottles and boxes to be discovered in the pagoda operating theater during the course of the day. Curiously, although there were a number of knives on the trolley beside the operating table, they were all clean: the knife used to slit Jude's stomach was not among them.

Also not found was Mr. Patrick Finnerty himself. Last seen in the early hours of the same morning by Nellie Moynihan, who was quite clear that he wanted her off the premises in a hurry, he seemed to have disappeared off the face of the earth. His jacket was draped over a chair in the study, and the pagoda garden door was hanging open when the police arrived. Where could he have gone, at such an hour, in his shirtsleeves, or perhaps in a surgical gown? And *how* had he gone? His green Bentley was still parked outside, as well as a Ford Focus, which turned out to be a hired car. Efforts continued throughout the day to trace him: to no avail.

By evening, the media had an approximate version of what had happened to Jude the previous night. The link was immediately made to the recent murder of his brother, Shadrack, and it was at once the lead item on all radio and television news bulletins. Superintendent Lennon appeared on TV to say that the police were very keen to have Mr. Patrick Finnerty "help them with their inquiries."

Penelope Finnerty heard the news on her car radio as she was motoring back to Dublin from West Cork. She pulled over and, with help from directory inquiries, she was soon talking to Inspector Quilligan. By eight o'clock that evening, she had met the inspector and told him all that she knew, down to the discovery of Shad's severed limb in her freezer.

"You may not believe this, Inspector, but I was actually on my way to Dublin today to tell you all of this. Only last night, perhaps at the very time when these terrible things were happening, I decided that I had to come and tell you what I knew."

"I believe you. Well, now you have done it, and we are grateful."

"Yes, but that poor boy Jude could so easily be lying dead today, the same as his brother—because of my delay."

Quilligan did not disagree. He shrugged gently, and said nothing.

Jude had been put in a private room at St. Vincent's Hospital, with an armed Garda on the door. His evidence was vital and Quilligan did not want any get well soon visits from Finnerty or anybody else, sent in to finish him off. The wound to his stomach was long but not deep: it was obviously a mere preliminary tracing for a much more serious incision which, for some reason, never got to happen. Three sutures were enough. The rest would heal quickly, held together with strong adhesive bandages. No permanent damage had been done. Jude had been heavily anesthetized. He would sleep it off. But if Finnerty had intended to give him the full contents of the syringe found smashed on the floor, he would never have woken up. The potassium chloride in the other syringe would have been quite superfluous.

By midday on the second day, the doctors let Quilligan in for "a few minutes." They warned him not to attempt to take a formal statement: the concentration needed would be too much for the boy. And anyhow, they added, at this early stage he would almost certainly forget or confuse things that he would remember more accurately later on. Quilligan kept it chatty and relaxed—and stayed for nearly an hour.

He was amazed by how much Jude had been able to work out

for himself. With the help of the little orphan boy, he had identified the person who had taken Shad away on the night when his foot was amputated and he'd died. His instinct to substantiate that identification by going back immediately to collect the cigarette packet discarded by the suspect was excellent. His reasoning about the rosary beads found in the funeral car had been balanced and rigorous. His midnight visit to the Finnerty home, and especially to the studio, though quite illegal, had been marked by the same intelligence and thoroughness, and he had been so much more open than experienced police officers to the possible and, as it now seemed, crucial relevance of the Golden Legend and the miracle of the severed leg. It all made Quilligan feel quite sheepish—which was in itself some achievement.

"Give up the restaurant job, Jude," he told the patient, "and join the Gardaí. You'd be commissioner in five years!"

Paradoxically, Jude could say very little about the night that had nearly cost him his own life. He told it like it happened, or at least how it began: Finnerty's telephone call, his own unwise decision to go and meet him, how he was suddenly overpowered in the car and anesthetized. That was about all he could say. He had the faintest memory of waking up on some stage with bright light shining down on him, of feeling pain, and of struggling with somebody.

"Nothing else? The window breaking?"

"In the car?"

"No, in the funeral home."

"I didn't even know I had been in the funeral home—until the nurses told me."

"Somebody broke that window and, in some way, put a sudden stop to Finnerty's evil work. Otherwise you would be dead."

"Yes. How did I escape? God is mighty!"

"I'm sure He is, but who broke the window? I doubt if God did

that in person. You see, that is what saved you. Somebody broke
the window. That started the alarm bell ringing. Finnerty had to
stop what he was doing. When he saw the police coming, he pan-
icked and ran away."

Jude thought about that for a while, then shook his head.

"I wonder, Inspector. Mr. Finnerty is a very tough guy, cheeky
man. He no go panic or run away. If the alarm go, he turn it off
quick, then he meet the police at the doorway and say that everything is fine fine. And also, even if the police does come inside,
he just puts a blanket over me. There must be many dead bodies
in that big funeral house. One more body under a blanket will
not make the police to think a fowl plays."

Quilligan laughed at the last bit but, once again, he was deeply
impressed with the way Jude could think things through. This was
the kind of person he loved to discuss a case with, somebody so
objective, even about a scenario where he nearly lost his own life.

Quilligan rang Molly late that night.

"Do you know what I think, Molly?"

"I will if you tell me, Jim."

"I think that Finnerty is dead."

"Oh. Why? Because he knew the game was up, so he offed
himself?"

"No, because somebody killed him."

"How do you know that?"

"We know that somebody interrupted him when he was carving up Jude."

"And how do you know that?"

"The garden gnome told me."

"What?"

"That garden-gnome—you saw the thing on the floor in the laboratory—it used to be in a sort of rockery just outside the window: I asked, and staff told me. So here is the scene: Somebody comes along, looks in the window, doesn't like what he sees, uproots the gnome, and crashes it through the window—to make Finnerty stop. I mean, to judge by the incision on Jude's belly, it was just in time; it was absolutely necessary to do something really quick."

"Okay, I'm with you. So . . ."

"So Finnerty now has *two* people he needs to kill: firstly, Jude, because Jude has worked out that Finnerty killed Shad, and Jude is going to tell *us* all about it next day. Finnerty knows that, and he is determined to stop him."

"And the second lucky person?"

"The second lucky person who Finnerty needs to kill is whoever it was that pushed the garden gnome through the window. He needs to kill that somebody because he or she has just seen Finnerty starting to murder Jude. Even if he thinks up some fatuous excuse for doing some minor surgery on the boy, he will not be able to finish killing Jude unless he kills the other guy also."

"Okay, so far I like it. But how does that show that *Finnerty* is dead?"

"Continue the story: Finnerty runs out the French doors carrying the knife he has in his hand, the very knife he has been slicing up Jude with—and which we have not been able to find. He chases this intruder with the knife—to do some more slicing. So the knife is missing and Finnerty is missing."

"Neat! So?"

"So Finnerty catches up with whoever he was chasing. They fight."

"And?"

"And the other guy wins. Simple as that! Which means that

Finnerty is lying, dead or disabled, not too far from his base."

"With the knife lying at his feet?"

"Yes, or possibly sticking out between his shoulder blades. We'll check it out tomorrow."

Jude got out of the hospital on the third day. The police drove him back to the restaurant, still nervous that someone might try to finish him off. He arrived to a hero's welcome, and in time for lunch. Everybody wanted to embrace him, to shake his hand, to congratulate him on having unmasked Shad's murderer and on his own miraculous escape from a similar fate. In African culture, bad fortune is often seen as a sign of displeasure on the part of the gods or of the ancestors. Jude's neighbors wanted him to know that, whatever evil had been visited on Shad and on himself, they were greatly respected and loved in this community and, by God's grace, they would triumph over evil in the end.

More and more people were arriving every minute. It seemed like everyone wanted to serve Jude's lunch, leaning over him from every side to propose the humble fare of the restaurant as the greatest gourmet treat, simply because it came from his own kitchen. Even Margot, whom everyone acknowledged as maîtresse d' hôtel on a normal day, and who was actually bringing the food, had to use her substantial haunches to clear a path through the melee from kitchen to table.

Pita, who had more reasons than anyone to shake Jude's hand, waited shyly to get near his table. He had told nobody about the trials and terrors of that night and, least of all, about the extraordinary role he had played in those events himself. Working his way unobtrusively, he was within a few feet of Jude's table, when he was spotted and pushed away contemptuously by Fat Isaac, who had appointed himself master of ceremonies for the occasion. He went back to wait patiently in his corner.

Everyone had eaten well. Kola nut—indispensable to any celebration—had been blessed and handed around, and there was even some palm wine and *kiki*, native gin, for those of sufficient age and dignity. Jude had told his story a dozen times, pointing out each time that, for the simple reason that he was asleep, he knew practically nothing about what happened on the night when he was captured. In particular, he did not know either who had interrupted Finnerty in his murderous assault, or where his assailant had disappeared to so mysteriously in the middle of the night.

"I cannot even swear that it *was* Finnerty who cut my belly open or who gave me those injections. I *know* it was him: who else could it be? But I was fast asleep. I did not actually *see* it."

"Call for you, Jude. Inspector Quilligan."

Jude went to the telephone. They followed him with their eyes, as if everyone knew that this was important. As he listened, and as they watched, his expression changed from polite interest to rapt attention, from mild surprise to open-eyed astonishment. He began to punctuate what he was hearing with short exclamations of amazement.

"Is that? . . . You mean it? . . . *eeeEEEeee!*"

This phase of wonder was soon followed by another change of tone, this time to vigorous denials, clearly rejoinders to suggestions the inspector was making at the other end of the line that Jude knew more than he was saying or might be covering up for something illegal, or even criminal.

"I no know . . . I was fast asleep . . . I hear nothing . . . I see nobody . . . nobody know where I am going when I leave restaurant that night . . . how can I tell someone where I am going when I no know it my very self! I think I am going out for ten minutes to talk to this man. Next thing, I wake up in hospital one day later. I don't tell the nurses where I have been: *they* tell *me*!"

He put down the phone. All eyes were on him. Instead of speaking, he stood motionless for several moments, as if trying to think through what he had just heard, as if struggling within himself to come to terms with something almost beyond belief. The room fell silent, tense, as when people do not know whether to hope or to fear.

Jude lifted his head.

"Pita!"

Everyone turned in surprise. The boy stood up. Jude called him again, quietly this time; was it with kindness, or respect, or even with something like awe? "Pita, come here."

People made space, and the boy came forward shyly, but his head was held high.

"Pita, did you follow me that night?"

"Yes."

"How did you know where to go?"

"When you talk with this man on the phone, I hear small. I know who he is and I guess then that he is calling you that side."

"But how do you go? It is far."

"I trek."

"You trek!"

"I trek, and then your God help me."

"How?"

"He send me more grease to my elbow . . . and one bicycle."

There were titters and murmurs of amazement.

"Did you break the window at his place with this statue-something?"

"This man is cutting up your body. So I crash the window with that this-thing. Then I stick my head and I shout him every bad talk I am knowing. He come out very angry and very too quick."

"He chased you . . . with the knife!"

"Yes now, but I run more better than him."

"But he catch you in the end?"

"At the end I am too tired. I can no run again. He is plunging at me with his knife. If he kill me, he turn around and go back kill you. So . . ."

The boy dropped one upturned hand into the other and shrugged his shoulders. Jude shook his head slowly from side to side in sheer wonder. He lifted his voice and spoke to the whole group who had listened to this exchange in amazement.

"This was Inspector Quilligan who telephone me. He say that Mr. Finnerty has been found in the bush, not far away from his own place. He is lying dead where he fall. He have one arrow sticking in his heart."

No human being worthy of the name applauds the killing of another person. But there were gasps of amazement and cries of admiration from all sides of the room for the fierce loyalty, the cool strategic sense, and the incredible courage of this tiny warrior, without whom Jude would undoubtedly have followed his brother to the grave.

Jude put his index finger under the boy's chin and lifted his head. Pita's lip trembled but his eyes were ablaze with a fearless and humble pride. Jude said not a word. He held up his hand. Pita crashed his hand into it. They gripped, turned, gripped again, linking and unlinking again and again, while the people punched the air, uttering over and over again the great cries with which one greets a mighty warrior.

EPILOGUE

QUILLIGAN WAS TEMPTED TO BELIEVE THAT THE WHOLE thing was a setup. According to this theory, Jude, from the moment he knew that Shad's murderer, if caught, would not be executed, had decided—on instructions from his ancestors no doubt—to take the law into his own hands. He would find the murderer. He would have him executed whilst, at the same time, giving himself a perfect alibi.

It was a lovely theory. All three elements were verified by the known facts. Jude *had* found the murderer. The murderer *had* been executed—and in a particularly non-European way. And Jude *did* have an excellent alibi. Just imagine the questions and answers!

"Where were you, Mr. Okafor, when Mr. Finnerty was being murdered?"

"I was lying on the flat of my back, stark naked, heavily anesthetized, and waiting for Mr. Finnerty to come back and finish murdering me."

Alibis don't come much better than that one.

A fourth element was, of course, required: a clever accomplice who would follow Jude closely as he passed into captivity, then into unconsciousness, carefully monitoring the whole proceedings, allowing Finnerty to inflict sufficient damage on Jude to make his villainous intentions clear, then intervening at exactly the right moment, first of all, to prevent him from doing too much harm, and then, to lead him instead to a suitable place for his own execution.

Quilligan was convinced that such an accomplice did exist. How else could it be that somebody should just happen to arrive in the middle of the night to this undertaker's private quarters, equipped conveniently with a bow and arrow, and decide on the spur of the moment to murder Finnerty, who himself happened to be engaged in trying to murder Jude? Nobody in his right mind could believe in such an accumulation of coincidences. There was somebody there that night who knew both what to expect and what to do.

On the other hand, the more he thought about it, the more Quilligan had to admit the frailties of his own theory. To begin with, he felt instinctively that Jude was a truthful person and that, when he had telephoned him that evening, only an hour or two before he was captured, he did really intend to meet the inspector the following morning and to tell him everything that he knew. The initiative for that night's hair-raising events had come from Finnerty. He, not Jude, was the one who was setting up a murder.

Besides, on Quilligan's theory, the risks being taken by Jude would be quite horrendous. He was to allow himself to be captured by a dangerous lunatic, to be rendered unconscious, and transported to an abbatoir where, unless his accomplice intervened at precisely the right moment, he would be slaughtered by lethal injections, disemboweled, and dismembered. If Finnerty had had the opportunity to make the deep incision that he had already marked out on Jude's abdomen, or if he had had the time to complete the injection of sodium thiopental which he had actually started, and if the accomplice had failed to arrive or to intervene exactly when he did, Jude would never have left that room alive.

Reluctantly but inevitably, Quilligan was obliged to abandon his theory. On Molly Power's advice, he settled on another hypothesis, that Jude had been followed by a fellow African, who had somehow discovered Finnerty's plan, or who had perhaps seen him overpowering Jude and driving away with him lying unconscious on the floor of his car. But if anybody had known of Finnerty's plan, he would surely have warned Jude about it. The field, therefore, was narrowed to somebody who had witnessed the kidnapping, who had grabbed his bow and arrow, and had followed Finnerty's car.

Whether it was an accomplice or somebody who had witnessed the kidnapping, Quilligan was convinced that such a person had to exist. He was also satisfied that many people in the African community knew perfectly well who that person was. But, try as he might, he could get nothing from any of them except nonstop dropping of one upturned open hand into the other upturned open hand, the ritual expression of perplexity, accompanied by protestations that only a Fulani nomad warrior would be able to perform this kind of execution, and that, seeing as there was no Fulani nomad warrior in Dublin at that particular time, the enigma was insoluble. Quilligan, his helpful informants implied, must incline his head before the awful decrees of Providence, of the ancestors, or of whoever it is that organizes these strange happenings. The police had heard this refrain more than once before. Quilligan *knew* that it was nonsense, but there was little he could do about it.

He checked out every African in the area with transport who could have made a quick decision to follow Finnerty's car. Tunde was in trouble on this score because he lived right next door to Jude, had a motorbike, and both he and the motorbike were absent on that very night. After a few false starts, when Tunde could not remember the name or the address of the B-and-B where he claimed to have spent that night in Kildare, he had traveled to Kildare with the police and found the premises. The proprietor, Mrs. Keyes, remembered him clearly, showed his name in her register for the correct date, and volunteered the invaluable information that the motorbike had spent the night, from 11:00 P.M. until eight o'clock the following morning, locked in her garage, at Tunde's request, for fear of robbers.

Fat Isaac, too, had trouble. He and his decrepit motor car had also been missing on that evening. Torn three ways—between the desire to be considered a warrior by the community, terror of being tortured by the police, and even more terror that people might find out where he really was that night—Fat Isaac told a mouthful of stupid lies which only made matters much worse. Eventually a certain fat lady from a traveling circus valiantly waddled forward and supplied the embattled Isaac with a truly substantial alibi—herself.

The African community richly repaid the orphan *pickin*'s loyalty to Jude. Nobody so much as breathed his name to the police. Quilligan and Molly often passed him in the street or met him in the restaurant or in other African houses as they went about their inquiries. He always had a beautifully disarming smile for them.

"Such a lovely child!" Molly enthused.

"Isn't he just?" Quilligan replied, "especially when you think of all he has been through."

Three months after the death of Patrick Finnerty, his widow asked Jude to call and see her. They had a long talk. She told him her whole story and apologized for not having alerted the police earlier to her husband's criminal activities. She added that Jude and his family were entitled to substantial compensation for the loss of their brother and for the injuries inflicted on Jude himself. Typically African, Jude said that Shad's death was God's will, and that he could not accept blood money. She then added the last detail, which she had so far omitted, about finding Shad's severed limb in her freezer. As she had expected, he was shocked. After a pause, he asked her:

"Do the police know about this?"

"They do."

"They never told me."

She looked at him in a strange way and smiled.

"Then I think that you should never tell them about Pita."

Jude stared at her astonished.

"How do you know about Pita?"

She did not answer his question. Instead she said,

"I buried Shad's poor remains in my garden. My suggestion is that you allow me to make a special casket for them. You and Pita must take them home to Nigeria and bury them in his own place. I will pay all the expenses of the journey. I will also pay you, quarterly, that is every three months, a certain sum of money, for as long as I live."

"You are very generous."

"No, I am not. What I am is a very wealthy woman who has been party to a great wrong, a wrong done to you, to your mother, and to your family. Money can never repair such injuries, but it is the only way I have of showing my regret. Also, quite frankly, it will make it easier for me to live with myself for whatever time is left to me. For my sake, if for no other reason, please accept what I am offering."

Eight years later, when Pita had grown to the dizzy height of five feet and seven inches and was halfway through medical school, Quilligan learned the full truth about how Patrick Finnerty had met his end. He picked it up from a casual remark of Peggy Breen, who had always assumed that he knew what Pita himself had told her in confidence so many years ago. Worried about what he should do, Quilligan asked his wife.

"Forget it, Jim!" she said. So he did—though he knew that he never would.